FROM HOUSEWIFE TO CUCKOLDRESS

FROM HOUSEWIFE TO CUCKOLDRESS

How I Took Sexual Control
of a Marriage in Crisis

ALEX HATHAWAY

fannypress

Seattle, WA

fannypress

Published by Fanny Press
PO Box 70515
Seattle, WA 98127

Cover design by Sabrina Sun
Contact: info@fannypress.com
Copyright ©2011 by Alex Hathaway

ISBN: 978-1-60381-490-4 (Paper)
ISBN: 978-1-60381-492-8 (ePub)

CHAPTER 1

THE TURNING POINT

~⦵~

M Y RELATIONSHIP WITH MY husband is going through a metamorphosis. Over a decade I have gone from being in awe of him, to being his sexual peer, to something else altogether. Something I don't fully understand. Something that is threatening to unravel us.

The turning point happened two years ago. Our eleven year old daughter is a gifted mathematician. She completed her high school curriculum by the time she was twelve. Sending her to a special math and science boarding school seemed like the best thing. My husband Dan and I missed her almost as much as she missed us, but a month into her new schooling, it was clear: we had made the right decision. Her phone calls became less frequent, and when Katherine did call, her voice carried the excitement kids get when they see the possibilities in front of them.

I think that, secretly, Dan and I both thought we'd fill our empty house with the kind of marathon sex sessions we hadn't had since Kathy was born. In recent years, our sex life has dwindled. I won't deny it's bothered me, but in every other way, our family makes sense. Bad thoughts were always filed away until the day they could no longer be ignored. Only problem: that day was now.

Our sex after Kathy left wasn't all that great. At first, I wrote it off to us being out of practice, but our rhythm was wrong. There was still love in our love making, but we weren't at risk of electrocution from the sparks.

One night when Dan and I were having sex, I found myself drifting off as Dan thrust into me. I can't remember what I was thinking about—groceries I shouldn't forget or some other mundanity. Then I snapped back, realizing he was about to come, pounding me harder. It felt good, but in kind of an observational, abstract way. "God, you selfish bitch!" flashed through my mind as he was trying to please me. That was when I heard a new voice in my head, a voice that was going to change a lot of things between us. *He's having trouble pleasing you … and he knows it!* the voice said quietly, diabolically. I stared intently into his face, realizing instantly it was true.

In the coming days, we kept having sex, but when I was honest with myself, I had to admit it was a pretty flat experience. Sometimes Dan would lick me to orgasm. I would come hard enough to fall asleep, but not hard enough to remember it in the morning. I've been told that you should always be honest when there is a block between your spouse and the sex you are having, but I kept quiet on this one, and so did he. Still, I chewed on that little voice in the back of my head … *he's having trouble pleasing you … and he knows it.* There was something cocky about it, something mean and nasty, something truthful. The best orgasm of that whole fall came with me masturbating to a rush of images, with that one thought repeating itself.

CHAPTER 2

DINNER PARTY

∽

WE PROBABLY WOULD HAVE gone on that way indefinitely, neither wanting to grapple with the implications, but life can take new turns. At the time, I was part of a massage therapy group. Massage was something I did before going to back to school to get my law degree. I liked to stay up on the techniques, and I enjoyed the women in the group. That fall, my friend Cheryl moved back and joined the group. Cheryl was a freewheeling woman, the kind you would never expect to settle down, the kind who would have been happier in a free love era long past. I was always fascinated with her lanky, chiseled body. She exercised a bit obsessively, but seeing her stomach muscles ripple through her leotard was pretty hot.

Cheryl never figured out much of a career path; moving around the country with a massage table—and no license— was about as far as she took it. But she knew her way around men, and unlike for some women, thirty-five was not an age that posed much difficulty for her. A while back, Cheryl had shacked up with a new guy. I didn't know much about him, except that he relocated to supervise the rollout of some cellular networks. I assumed when she talked about her new guy—Eddie—that he was rich and willing to fund her funky lifestyle. I pictured a flabby, overweight businessman who spent his way into women like Cheryl. When Cheryl invited us to a dinner party at Eddie's place, I agreed, mostly out of curiosity. Plus, Dan always had a thing for Cheryl; he wouldn't object to an evening in her company.

Dan had to run back to the car to get my jacket, so when I knocked, I was standing there by myself, a bit shivery in the October air, when Eddie opened the door. I gasped audibly when I saw him. If you've seen that show *Mad Men*, and you can conjure up the image of Don Draper, that's not too far off from what I saw before me. I soon found out Eddie was a tri-athlete who worked only half-time. He spent the rest of his time training, and he looked the part. Six foot three or so, 220 pounds, and ridiculously arrogant. While I stood in the doorway waiting for Dan to catch up, Eddie's eyes undressed me with impunity, making me feel like he had already cheated on Cheryl. I fought the urge to slap Eddie as we made the introductions.

We went inside, and dinner began. As the four thirty-something couples at the table bantered on about work and politics and babysitters, I felt on firmer ground. Eddie had an irritating way of expressing his opinions as facts. I was proud to see Dan run intellectual circles around him, not only showing a more sophisticated world view, but taking the time to listen and ask questions of the women at the table. Dan really was a man to admire in these situations; he had this beautiful way of making everyone in a conversation feel like they had a worthwhile viewpoint, as opposed to conversation-blasting bullhorns like Eddie. *Dan is such a good listener*, I thought to myself. *I'm so lucky to be spending my life with a true partner rather than a macho windbag like Eddie.* That thought settled in nicely.

But then the rebuttal came: *right, Linda, but when you can fuck a woman as well as Eddie, it doesn't really matter how sensitive you are, now does it?* Grrr ... that voice again. I tuned it out quickly. What proof did I have that Eddie was good in bed? "He's probably one of those two-minute men, getting his rocks off and falling to sleep," I reassured myself. *Ha ... keep telling yourself that. When Eddie undressed you at the door, he was already thinking about what you would look like coming like crazy on his cock.*

Dammit! The voices were getting harder to drown out, and it didn't make sense. "Act like jerks, fuck like jerks" had always been my experience. *Dan really cares about what I like, and that's why I love him. But look at Cheryl's face. Look at the glow and the smile. See that? That's because Eddie is fucking her brains out—with his huge cock!*

Okay, that does it! I excused myself and got up from the table. I went to the bathroom, thoroughly flustered, with only myself to blame. I splashed cold water on my face, trying to dim the flush without washing off my makeup. *What are you thinking? Talking to yourself about your friend's boyfriend's cock? And you don't even know how big it is anyway—not that size matters!* A couple more moments freshening up and I felt more like myself. But as I walked back to the table, I felt a wetness between my legs, sliding a bit as I walked. It was a nasty, slutty feeling, one that thrilled me more than I cared to admit.

I was grateful to be wearing jeans and a thick pair of underwear for the cold. My nipples were rigid and achy, poking their way through my bra and my tight sweater. I might have been embarrassed about that in the past, but for some reason, tonight I wasn't. When I sat down, I glanced at Cheryl, and yes, dammit, she did look happy.

Dinner was over. Two couples left; it was down to the four of us. We were drinking coffee spiked with Amaretto when Cheryl suddenly chimed in with, "Who's up for the hot tub?"

Silence ensued. Dan and I looked at each other. "Well, we don't actually have suits ...." I volunteered half-heartedly.

"Neither do we," said Cheryl. "Well, we do, but we never use them. Au natural baby!!" (Cheryl had a tendency to say hippy dippy nails-on-chalkboard things like that). She also had a tendency to get her way.

"C'mon guys, the pool's right outside the patio door. You can just jump in!" Cheryl piped up.

I looked at Eddie, and could have sworn I saw a smirk flash across his face. Jeez I was imagining everything now!

"Okay, let's do it!" I said impulsively. Dark, unspeakable motivations were driving me. Then I backtracked, realizing I never speak for Dan.

"Dan," I turned to him, "my shoulder *has* been a little achy; I do think the hot tub would do the trick."

"I'll go turn the heat up," Eddie said as he left the room. Cheryl busied herself in the kitchen getting drinks while Dan and I cleared coffee cups. We told Cheryl we'd wash a few while they got the tub ready. I was aware of Dan's apparent discomfort, but put it out of my head in a dismissive way.

When we walked into the living room that looked onto the patio, I was disappointed to see Cheryl was already in the hot tub. No use denying it—I really enjoyed looking at her athlete's body. Eddie had his back to the door; I could see the muscles rippling up and down his back. He threw his towel down, his ass and leg muscles shimmying as he lowered himself into the water.

Dan seemed self-conscious. He wasn't much of an exhibitionist—he actually dimmed the living room lights before taking off his clothes and stepping quickly into the water. For some reason, that *bad* voice in my head told me, *show off your sexy body a little*. I took off the towel I had wrapped around me, and despite the cold, took a bit of time putting it down, pretending to look for a dry spot.

"Damn girl!" Cheryl yelled out.

I thought Cheryl would be impressed. In the last two years since I'd hung out with her, I'd lost almost fifteen pounds. I'm five foot eight inches tall and about 130 pounds now—maybe ten pounds heavier than during my college years, but a lot lighter than I had been since. I was always a perfectionist about my weight, but the good thing about 130 pounds is that my tits were really big—almost a D cup and a lot bigger than Cheryl's.

Cheryl always appreciated my "old school '70s rack" as she put it, or sometimes, my "bodacious rack" or my "boy magnets." They weren't as perky as they once were, but at thirty six, they had held up pretty well—though I can't lie: I was dreading another ten years of aging there. My ass still felt big to me, but I knew that my wide hips were another part of my body that men ogled and Cheryl herself envied.

I sauntered towards the hot tub—there's no other way of putting it. And there was that voice again. *You're showing off; you love teasing guys with your hot body and getting whatever you want.* What a horrible thing to think! Considering how hard I have worked to become a woman who has many great attributes—not just looks—I didn't like thinking about my hip power. But there it was. Was I really just a slut at heart? A slut for guys like Eddie, that bad, bad voice said as I lowered myself into the tub.

CHAPTER 3

HOT TUB REVELATIONS

❦

SOON WE WERE LOW on drinks, and the hot tub was too damn pleasant to get out of. Cheryl told the guys to fetch us gin and tonics. A hesitant look flashed across Dan's face, but when Eddie got out of the hot tub, Dan did too. It only took ten seconds for them to walk into the living room from the deck, but in the slow motion of my head, it took much longer.

I struggled to stifle a gasp as I saw Eddie's big soft cock literally flopping from side to side. It hung arrogantly down his thighs like a python. In contrast, Dan's penis was small and boyish. I felt a primal flash of embarrassment, as if I had settled for a second-tier male while my friend Cheryl had scored the alpha. The moment passed, but Eddie's big flopping cock got bigger and bigger inside my mind.

Out of my daze, I realized that Cheryl was looking over at me and smiling wickedly.

"Linda ... Linda ...." She snapped her fingers as I turned to her.

"It's amazing the differences in the male anatomy, huh?" she asked. I wanted to say "Yes!" emphatically, but felt the need to defend my husband.

"Well, you know Cheryl, some guys are grow-ers and some are show-ers," I said in an unconvincing way.

"Oh Pleeeeease ..." said Cheryl. "There's no way Dan's little penis is anywhere near Eddie's cock in size. No way."

I couldn't believe Cheryl's frankness, but then, that's how Cheryl always was—I guess I had just forgotten. "Cheryl, you don't know that! Dan is a fine size." I was starting to get mad. Cheryl was acting like a superficial sorority girl, judging my husband against jerky Eddie.

"Sure, whatever you say," said Cheryl, smiling to herself. I noticed that my right hand was casually moving between my thighs. I could feel a tingling between my legs, a desire to rub and caress.

When the guys came back out, the size contrast was again astonishing, but I forced myself to look away. We all got back to talking; I felt a sigh of relief when the moment passed. Still, I could feel some warm/happy sensations lingering between my thighs.

Then Cheryl shook up the evening. "Eddie, honey, can you do me a favor? Linda and I were having an argument and I need to show her something ... sit up please."

Eddie was only too happy to sit on the edge of the tub. While I sat there in a state of shock, Cheryl picked up Eddie's big ropey cock with one hand and started to jack it. Slowly but surely, Eddie's soft cock started to grow and harden. Still bent, it was starting to straighten and swell.

"That's it," Cheryl cooed as she jacked it a bit more aggressively. I was struck by the cocky look on Eddie's face. Eddie's dick was at least eight inches and as thick as my forearm; it looked monstrous and obscene. It wasn't smooth and pretty like Dan's; it was a big fat monstrous half-alive thing ... and I was getting wetter and wetter staring at it. *That, Linda, is the most masculine thing you have ever seen,* that wicked voice inside me said.

"That's it, Eddie, show them that big cock of yours, show them how huge you get for me!" Cheryl was getting kind of nasty and didn't seem to care. She got up and kneeled on the other side of Eddie so we would have a better view. Before we knew it, she was jacking that huge cock, presenting it to us. Even though his dick had two hands on it, its big head and part of its shaft still pushed out.

"Oh, Ed, what a beautiful huge cock you have," Cheryl cooed. "Show them how hard you can get .... Show them what you take care of this pussy with ...."

I couldn't believe how Cheryl was talking, but we all had a few drinks in us. In this drunken state, it felt natural for Cheryl to be paying homage to this big cock right in front of us. I looked over at Dan, and he was as fixated on the scene as I was. I couldn't blame him; Cheryl's beautiful back muscles were rippling in the deck lights. It was like watching two cougars, two perfectly muscled animals, prepare for sex.

Something came over me, and I reached underwater between Dan's legs. I found his cock rock hard, as hard as I could remember feeling it. I started stroking it while watching the action. *This turns him on.* The thought seared into my brain. Looking at Cheryl jacking Eddie's fat cock with two hands made me compare my hand on Dan's cock. *Cheryl was right. Eddie's cock is MUCH bigger. She can't even handle him with two hands, meanwhile, your hand easily swallows up Dan's hard little dick.* ARGH! That might have been the cruelest, most politically incorrect thought I've ever had. But there it was. And the truth of it was undeniable.

"Oh Eddie," Cheryl said. "Stroking you is making my pussy so wet ... I want to fuck you right in front of them ... feel you filling me up so good ... show them how you split my pussy open ...." Eddie just groaned. Cheryl was jacking him with one hand and rubbing his big ball sack with the other. I couldn't take it anymore ... with Cheryl talking like that. I had to put my own hand inside me. I touched my crotch with my left hand and felt a massive jolt up and down my body. *You're such a nasty slut, oh, you are ....*

"On second thought, let's save that for later," said Cheryl. Perhaps she was shy about fucking Eddie right in front of us— we had never had that kind of swinging friendship in the past. I felt secretly disappointed.

But then she said: "No, let's make you come instead! I wanna see that dick come!" *Oh yes, so do I, so do I* …. Cheryl started stroking the shaft with both hands again. "Two hands, Eddie," Cheryl said, "Just the way you like it."

"Ohhh …" Eddie moaned.

"You love it when girls worship that big cock of yours … don't you … don't you!"

"Ohhh …" was all Eddie could say ….

"You love it, right?" Cheryl demanded, increasing the pace.

"Oh yes!" yelled Eddie.

"That's right."

As Cheryl jerked Eddie's cock faster and faster, I worked Dan's cock furiously with my hand as well. The look of lust on Dan's face as he watched the action spurred me on. Before long Eddie's dick was coming, squirting again and again, launching big long ropes of cum across Cheryl's tits and chest.

Dan's cock started twitching in my hand and I knew he was coming also, but I didn't say anything because he was coming underwater. After a few spurts, Dan was done. I was a bit embarrassed he had come in the hot tub, but Cheryl was busy looking for a towel and didn't notice. She rubbed a hand towel all over her upper body.

"Jeez Eddie, you ruined another towel! That big dick has a lot of cum in it!" She teased him. The towel was pretty much drenched in cum. *It would take Dan about ten loads to drench a towel like that*—my last perverted thought of the night. After the guys came, things got a bit quiet. It was getting late. We all got out of the tub. The sexual tension had dissipated a bit; awkwardness kicked in. We all dressed quickly.

Before I left, I pulled Cheryl aside. "Sorry; Dan came in the hot tub."

"Not a problem," Cheryl smiled back teasingly. "It wouldn't be the first time ...." I thought she was going to say something else, but she must have thought better of it because her voice trailed off, her playful smirk lingering.

CHAPTER 4

GIRL TALK

∽

AFTER WE GOT HOME, Dan and I didn't talk about what had happened. I'm not sure if we were in a state of shock, but we ended up in bed ready to sleep, couples in a domestic rhythm. Dan fell asleep quickly, but I didn't. I was way too horny. I ended up working myself to an amazing come just fingering myself, hot memories of the evening flashing through my head.

A few days later, Dan and I had sex. It was good, but after Dan went to sleep, I found myself masturbating again, something I never used to do. Always it was the memories of that night, flashing through my head in a forbidden jumble. Cheryl and Eddie had been out of town since that night, so they were safely removed from our reality, but masturbating after Dan went to sleep did feel shameful and slutty. For a couple of weeks, this became my new ritual—good sex with Dan, then an even better goodnight orgasm after he went to sleep.

Two weeks after the hot tub night, the phone rang. Cheryl was back in town. Eddie was away on business, so she invited me over. I wasn't sure I should go. Some good girl part of me told me not to, but I went anyway, my dirty thoughts egging me on.

Spurred on by hot espressos from her new espresso machine, brewed a bit too strong, we chatted about many things, but *that* special evening soon became the main topic.

"So have you thought about it?" asked Cheryl.

"What?" I asked, knowing what she meant, but shy.

"About that night."

"Yes," I admitted, relief sweeping over me. "I think about it a lot."

"I thought so," smiled Cheryl in a reassuring but naughty way. "When girls see Eddie's cock in action, they can't easily put it out of their minds."

"Oh, it's not that!" I said impulsively.

"Umm … yes it is," Cheryl said.

A moment of silence, then, "Yeah, you're right," I confessed.

"It's totally normal," Cheryl said. "You're not the first girl who has left here with Eddie's cock burned into her brain and an itch between her legs."

I had a sudden impulse to put down my drink and flee Cheryl's house, never to return. I almost did. But I also felt a surge of tingly wetness between my legs, and that wanton sensation was hard to resist. The conversation was pulling me somewhere I had never been. I dreaded what it might mean, but I wanted the stirring within me to continue.

"To tell you the truth, it's all I think about. After Dan goes to sleep, I masturbate while recalling that night."

"That's better," said Cheryl. "But it's not just that night you masturbate about. You masturbate about my boyfriend's big cock." Another twitch between my legs.

"Yes. Yes I do." Silence. "I'm sorry."

"Don't be," said Cheryl. "I'm very secure in my relationship with Eddie. And Linda, you should know," she continued, "it's very normal for a woman who is dating a man with a small penis to wonder what it would be like to be filled and stretched by a man like Eddie. Size is not just a manufactured male insecurity. You know that by now, right?"

I blushed. "But Dan isn't small .... I'm happy with his size."

"Honey, sorry to break it to you, but Dan has a small dick. I'm guessing it's not much more than five inches. When it comes to fucking, the difference between a cock like Dan's and a cock like Eddie's is almost unfair, believe me."

I couldn't stop blushing. I didn't want what she said to be true, but the lusty part of me feared it was.

"Linda, I want you to do something for me," Cheryl said.

"What?"

"I want you to fuck Eddie. And I want to be there."

Violent vaginal twitch, starting between my legs and coursing through my body.

"What?"

"Yeah," said Cheryl. "I like to share Eddie from time to time. I especially like to share him with beautiful girls like you who have never had a chance to experience a man like him."

Another surge. But a problem.

"I could never do that to Dan," I said.

"Oh, yes you could." said Cheryl. "And besides, Dan would be there too."

Umm .... "What?"

"Yeah, Dan would be there too, watching you, and he'd be even more turned on than you."

I looked at Cheryl with disbelief. "Dan would never stand for that," I said confidently.

"Oh, don't be so sure," Cheryl said. "Guys with small penises fear they can't satisfy their women—that size really does matter—and they crave a chance to find out in person."

I had nothing to say; what she said made no sense.

"Think about it," said Cheryl. "Has Dan ever made you come with his cock?"

"Oh, all the time!" I said quickly.

"By that you mean," Cheryl said, "that he's made you come

without using a finger on your clit while he was fucking you?"

I had to think about that. "Yes, a couple of times." She was right, not very often. "But lots of women can't come through penetration!" I said, quoting the popular sexual wisdom.

"Well, that may be true in some cases," said Cheryl. "But Eddie has fucked well over a hundred women, and he can only think of a few that didn't come on his cock. And two of those were from his teens, when he didn't know how to use what he had, and they were tight and scared."

Silence.

"Those are pretty good odds," Cheryl persisted. "And you know what else?" she asked.

"What?"

"Guys like Dan get off on watching their women get fucked if they are given the chance. Just think about that night in the hot tub. Dan's little dick was rock hard, wasn't it? Watching me jack Eddie's big cock."

She was right: Dan's cock had been rock hard that night.

"I know all about these kinks," says Cheryl. "I attract a lot of guys with small penises who get off on my dominant tendencies. I know what gets to them. Dan was hard because he was thinking about what you would look like coming all over Eddie's big cock."

I could only sit, absorbing this outrageous scenario. And while my head was grappling with it, my wetness was increasing. I could feel my lips parting and swelling between my legs.

"If you want proof, just ask Dan about that night. Ask him if, when you were jacking Dan off in the hot tub, he was thinking about Eddie fucking the shit out of you."

I had to leave. The talk was overwhelming me; my head was spinning. Her words were so farfetched …. Surely this boiled down to more than penis size …. *But why does talking about it turn you on so much?*

CHAPTER 5

SNEAKY MASTURBATION

I AVOIDED CHERYL'S PHONE calls for a while. A month went by, then another. I stuck with my masturbation routine. But one weird thing did happen. The sex Dan and I were having deteriorated again, going from good to only okay. Meanwhile, my masturbation sessions were becoming more intense than ever. I found myself checking out guys at the strangest places—supermarkets, gas stations, doctor's offices. *This can't keep up*, I thought. *If you don't do something, you are going to cheat on Dan with some strange guy.* Another dark thought came—from outer space it seemed—that rang oddly true. *This is how marriages fizzle—the slow fade, the secrets, the repression that finds expression elsewhere.*

Some turning points appear like a big old fork in the road, but others sneak up on you. In my case, the next one came in the middle of the night. Dan was asleep and I was masturbating, taking my slow delicious time, working my way around my pussy lips, in lazy circles toward my clit.

"Do you do this a lot?" asked Dan. He was wide awake.

I didn't know what to say. A part of me wanted to just say

"no" and bury the whole thing, let it die. But I wasn't sure it ever would.

"Yes, I do," I said. There it was.

"Does our sex not satisfy you anymore?" Dan asked, pain in his eyes.

I felt so bad that my first response was apologetic reassurance. Apologize! Put him at ease! Comfort him! But another force in me said *NO!* and led me down a different path.

"Dan, can I ask you something?"

"Yes, Linda ... of course."

"Do you remember that night at Cheryl's?"

"Uh, how could I forget?"

"Well, you know when I was masturbating you underwater, and Cheryl was jacking Eddie's cock?"

"Uh, yeah, duh!"

"Well, can I ask you what you were thinking about while I jacked you off?"

"Sure," Dan said. "I was thinking about how hot and crazy that whole scene was. And I hope you're not mad, but I was really getting off on the view of Cheryl's ass in the deck lights. Your body is amazing, but it was really something to see her hips swaying in heat like that."

I lay there for a moment, taking in what he had said. I almost let it go. But something stopped me. *Your marriage is at stake tonight*, that voice insisted. *Your sexual confidence is at stake tonight.* One more. *Your future orgasms are at stake tonight.*

Some kind of sex demon must have taken control of me, because before I knew it, I was straddling Dan's naked body, tits swaying in his face.

"That's not all, is it Dan?"

"What do you mean?" Dan said smiling up at me, amused by my sudden aggression.

"That's not all you thought about that night."

"What else did I think about?" asked Dan in his clever, joking way.

"You thought about me. You thought about me fucking Eddie."

"I did?" Dan asked with amusement.

"Yes Dan, you did."

I grabbed Dan's cock in my hand, then looked down at him and said, "You thought about Eddie fucking me with his big cock."

Dan looked surprised, accused. But his cock twitched noticeably in my hand.

"Didn't you Dan? Didn't you? You thought about that big cock all up inside me!"

"Yes!" Dan finally called out, excited, relieved. His cock twitched harder in my hand as I stroked him. "Yes, Linda, I did!"

"That's better ..." I purred, savoring my control. "That feels good, doesn't it Dan?"

"Oh God yes," he said as I continued to stroke.

"Well Dan, guess what?"

"What?"

"I thought about it, too."

"You did?"

"Yes. And I have to tell you, I can't stop thinking about it."

His cock twitched some more, growing harder.

"Dan, I don't want to lie to you anymore. If I lie to you, if I don't tell you everything, something bad is going to happen to us."

"I don't want you to lie either."

"Okay. That is good, that is very good." I felt relief, but also a resurgence of wickedness.

I continued: "But Dan, I want your whole truth also."

"Okay," he said, not yet realizing what that would mean.

"Dan, I can't stop thinking about Eddie's big cock inside me. It's awful, but it's true. I think about it all the time. Sometimes it makes me ashamed, but it gives me the biggest orgasms ...."

I stopped stroking him for a moment.

Dan looked upset, betrayed, confused.

I rolled off him as the sexy vibe dissipated. Where was this going?

"Linda?" Dan asked.

"Yes."

"Can we talk about this tomorrow? I need to think."

"Okay," I said, and I went to sleep, not horny but unsettled. I did feel a little lighter.

CHAPTER 6

THE SIZE OF IT

❦

"LINDA?" IT WAS HOURS later, still before dawn. Dan had woken me up; the lamp next to his bedside was on.

"Linda, I need to talk to you."

"Sure Dan." I rolled over on my side to face him.

"Linda, I have to tell you something." A short pause. "I can't stop thinking about it, either."

"What?"

"About Eddie and his big cock, and how much I wanted to see him fuck you with it."

"Really?" I said.

"Yeah," Dan said. "It feels good to admit it. I have jacked off many times in my office since that night."

"Really??"

The sex surged back into the room. Sensing it, I slid on top of him again. "Really Dan?"

"Yeah."

I grabbed his cock again.

"Dan, thank you!! Thank you for being honest with me …. I know that wasn't easy."

"Oh God …" Dan moaned as I stroked his cock.

"Dan, can I ask you something?"

"Yes."

"Did you feel small next to Eddie?"

"What do you mean?"

"When you were standing next to Eddie, did you feel like, you know, your penis was small?"

"Well …."

"Because Dan, I have to say, I did." *Something bad in me had taken over.* "I've never thought of your dick as small, but seeing it next to Eddie's big cock, I was shocked at the difference."

Dan seemed dazed, but his face was contorted with horniness, and his cock was twitching like mad.

"Hmm, Cheryl was right," I said, smiling.

"About what?" said Dan, surprised that I mentioned her.

"She said guys with small penises (*here we go!*) guys like you, Dan—like hearing about how small they are compared to studs like Eddie."

And there it was: Dan's penis shot up into its hardest state. I had never seen such a quick transition from soft to hard.

"Dan, that's it!"

"What?" he said.

"You like it! You like knowing that your cock is small and Eddie's is so much bigger. It turns you on."

Dan's expression was tortured, but horny, too.

I started stroking him faster, relishing my control. My determination not to cheat on Dan but *to take what was mine* within the relationship was changing everything.

"Guess what else, Dan? Cheryl says that Eddie's big cock does feel fantastic inside her, that size really, *really* matters."

"Ohhhh," Dan moaned.

"She said it feels *so* much better than smaller cocks … smaller cocks like yours."

"Ohhhh …" Dan moaned.

"You wanna cum, Dan? You wanna cum?"

"Ohhhh …."

"Are you my dirty boy, thinking about Eddie's big cock inside me?"

"Yessss!"

"You want me to stroke it, stroke that little cock while you think about Eddie's big cock filling my pussy up?"

"Oh God, yes!" Dan cried out. God he was hard; he was ready to burst.

"Let me see it Dan! Let me see that little dick cum! Squirt for me!"

"Ohhhh!"

"See if you can make a big load like Eddie's!!"

"Cummming …!"

Dan spurted his load in my hand. And that was it.

After Dan's cum, my emotions were mixed. But I wasn't sorry. I felt an odd sense of relief. Sexual control was, I guess, mine for the taking. Feeling no need to come, I started to nod off. A few minutes later, Dan curled up against me. For the first time in a while, our closeness felt unforced. *You didn't tell him.* Tell him what? *About Cheryl's offer. Another time*, I told myself, *another time.* I slept soundly in Dan's arms, more soundly than I had in a long time.

CHAPTER 7

THE DILEMMAS OF CHEATING

∞

THINGS CHANGED AFTER THAT night, but not in the way I had anticipated. "The talk" had released the steam from the pressure cooker. Basking in the relief of that, Dan and I had some of the best sex we'd had in months. We were honest like never before—sharing fantasies we used to keep to ourselves, confiding insecurities, being bluntly honest about what we wanted. The result was an intimacy I thought had been lost to us.

I didn't talk to Cheryl much, not for a few months. We always seemed to have other plans when she and Eddie invited us over. I started to feel like I didn't need to do anything more to threaten or save our marriage. Maybe all I'd really wanted was the honesty we had achieved.

About four months after that night with Eddie and Cheryl, I ran into a mutual friend, Christine, who had been happily married for ten years. We ran into each other at the car dealership and before long, we were making plans to go out for dinner and drinks. A girls' night out ensued and we were drinking more than we should. We ended up on the balcony of an open-air brewpub.

"Linda, I want to tell you something; I *have* to tell you something."

"Sure, what?" I said.

"I cheated on Bill."

"What? You guys have the best marriage I know!"

"It was a few years ago, and I have never forgiven myself," said Christine.

"Wow," I said.

"The thing that bothers me the most is that I don't really regret it, I mean—I feel guilty but I kinda don't."

I didn't really know what to say. "Well, I'm glad you could talk to me about it."

"The thing is—it was really the best sex I'd ever had in my life. Once I started, I just couldn't stop."

I smiled at her, trying to encourage her, curious.

"Actually, I think you know the guy. He's dating Cheryl now." *No!!*

"Eddie?" I asked. I was suddenly angry and jealous, for no good reason. "You fucked Eddie?"

"Shhh!" Christine said, looking around, but there was no one near us. "Yes, you could say that. Or, maybe I should say that he fucked me. He almost fucked me right out of my marriage."

I wanted to know more, but I was also really mad at her. After an awkward silence, I finally blurted out: "And why was the sex so good?"

"Well," Christine said, "Eddie has an incredible cock and he really knows what to do with it."

Mmm ... .

"I mean, Linda, I've had two kids, but when Eddie put his cock inside me, I felt like a virgin again. I've never felt so full before, wow! At first, anyway ..." Christine said wistfully.

My legs started to twitch; I resisted the urge to rub them up against the balcony.

"The first time we did it, I swore I would never do it again," Christine went on. "But I kept calling him. And he kept on fucking me. God I have *never* ...."

I was fighting off images of Eddie pounding Christine, bending her over a kitchen table or a countertop, pushing her big round ass in the air, and letting that mother of two just *have it* till she screamed for mercy. God it was all I could do not to excuse myself and go downstairs, lock myself up in a stall and masturbate. I could feel my panties cling.

"Anyway ...." Christine's voice drifted off. "My husband could never fuck me like that, never. I mean, he tries, but he doesn't have Eddie's natural advantages ... and Eddie, he just *takes control* of a woman's body. My husband, he's kind of shy around me, asking me what feels good. Eddie just takes me, dominates me .... I have never felt anything like it."

"Really?" I asked, trying to draw her out even more, trying not to clue her in on how much her story had nailed my own preoccupations.

"Yeah," Christine said. "And the thing is, my husband is a pretty decent size. He's about seven inches, but he's kind of thin down there and Eddie, he's so thick, so long."

I couldn't help but go back in my mind to Dan's cock, wondering how it compared to Christine's husband's, if they were different as lovers.

"The best thing," Christine said, "was feeling Eddie come so deep inside me, just drenching me. I have never felt more like a woman. I'm still shocked he didn't knock me up. I have no idea how my birth control killed all that sperm."

"So how did it end?" I asked.

"It ended in a humiliating way, at least for me. I started to fall for him. He never called me, knowing I couldn't get enough of him ... and I'd always call. I hated the control he had over me, and the feelings I was starting to have for that asshole. Anyway, this one time I came over to his place without calling, and he was fucking a college girl from next door. I actually stayed and watched them fuck. I took a dirty pleasure out of watching him just ruin this woman's pussy for her boyfriend. I don't know why, maybe because young women settle for the wrong guys so often. But I felt betrayed, too, even though he had never promised me anything. Heck, I was married."

"How did you know her boyfriend had a small dick?" I asked, seeking out the information my mind and pussy craved.

"Well, she couldn't stop talking about it. She was yelling while he was fucking her, and she kept on saying that his dick felt so much better than her boyfriend's little one. At one point he started teasing her about it, and she finally laughed and yelled, 'no more small dicks for this pussy!' And he kept on putting it to her. You know, I couldn't blame her. If I could go back to college, I wouldn't put up with small dicks. Seems like most girls don't these days.

"But you know what?" Christine continued. "I realized I couldn't destroy my marriage over it either. If Eddie hadn't been so open about seeing other girls, if he had fallen for me, too, I honestly don't know what would have happened. But I couldn't share him. I guess that kind of woke me up to what I had. I mean, my husband isn't small, and he's good in bed—sometimes he's great—and there's more to life than sex. You know?" I wasn't sure if she was trying to convince me, or herself.

"Did you ever think about telling your husband?" I asked.

"Yeah ..." said Christine. "I tried to once, but he just said, 'We all make mistakes.' It was a beautiful moment, and that's when I knew I had to put this behind me. I couldn't lose my husband over this cock-chasing stupidity. And you know what? My desire for Eddie did fade ....

"I guess Eddie will always leave me with a complicated sense of right and wrong," she continued, as if knowing what I needed to hear. "I knew what I was doing was wrong, but in the moment, nothing could have felt more right, like I totally deserved to be fucked that well. I guess the good part is that guys like Eddie don't come along that often. Most of the guys who hit on me are cocky blowhards who can't get a woman in the mood. Nowadays, I focus on my man and my family and that's … that's really it."

The talk slowed down, as both got lost in our own thoughts. Driving home that night, I felt restless, uncertain.

CHAPTER 8

UNSETTLING TIMES

∽

THE NEXT MONTH WAS an unsettling time. The sex between Dan and me was again bland, uninspired. I found myself masturbating at night, having all kinds of nasty thoughts, usually centered around Eddie. Sometimes I would get mad at Christine—why did she have to say what she did? I was contaminated with jealousy but also wary of her story. Things with Eddie had not ended well. Whatever Pandora's box had been opened needed to be shut. But with the shutting of that box came the dulling of the marriage. Was there any way out?

One day I got sick of my head games and just called Cheryl. When I told Dan I was having lunch with Cheryl, he gave me a curious look. Cheryl's offer was something we had never discussed, the one exception to my vow of honesty. Cheryl and I ended up in a bustling diner, so I couldn't really talk to her the way I wanted. But I asked her to go on a walk afterwards.

When I got back that evening, I had renewed clarity. I wanted to talk to Dan, but he fell asleep early. I thought about letting him sleep through the night, but then that urge welled up inside me. I didn't want to masturbate again. I turned on my bedside lamp and woke him.

"Dan, are you awake?"

"I am now …" Dan said with a sleepy yawn.

"Dan, I have to tell you something."

"Yeah?"

"Dan, I haven't been totally honest with you."

Dan looked over at me, disappointment in his eyes. I could tell he suspected I had cheated on him.

"Dan, Cheryl made me an offer—after that night in the hot tub."

"An offer?"

"Yeah. She said that I could have sex with Eddie, one time, on the condition that you agree, and both of you get to watch."

"What?"

"She insists on these rules because she doesn't want to hurt our marriage. She wants to help us."

Dan's look was skeptical.

"Cheryl tells me that honesty is a *must* in these situations."

I paused, took a deep breath.

"She's worried that if I don't do something like this within the relationship, I'm going to do it outside the relationship."

Dan was silent.

"She thinks I'm going to cheat on you sooner rather than later, and Dan, I'm worried that she's right."

More silence.

"This isn't going to be easy for me to say or for you to hear. Cheryl thinks now that I've heard what a difference size makes to a woman's pleasure, I'm going to have to see for myself. I'm going to be tempted to find out if that is what is missing from our sex."

"Do you really think it matters that much?" Dan asked, hurt and defensive.

"Well, I don't know. But here's what I do know: Cheryl told me that of the more than 100 women Eddie has slept with, only three have not had vaginal orgasms through penetration— each and every time they had sex. And in all the times you and I have had sex, I've only had a vaginal orgasm a couple of times."

I felt a mean desire to lay it on a little more. "And Cheryl says she usually comes on Eddie's big cock multiple times every time they have sex.

"But there's more ..." I said. "I can't put a finger on it, but there's something about Eddie, something I'm drawn to. It's not love; I don't think I could ever love him. But it's something very animal, something I need ... something ... I don't know how to say this ... something I'm not getting in our marriage."

Dan was quiet, but the look on his face was not just hurt anymore. I could see jealousy, and horniness as well. *No looking back—see this through.*

"Cheryl wants to create a supportive environment for you to see someone please me in a way that, according to her, you can't. She says it's not your fault, but your penis is too small to fill a mature woman's pussy. Vaginal orgasms are about being filled and stretched, and honey, that's just not something you can do."

I saw Dan's cock twitching under the sheets. I pulled the sheets down and wrapped my hand around his cock.

"I do worry about it," Dan said.

"What?" I asked, drawing him out.

"That I'm too small for you, that you need more, that somehow this is going to ruin what we have between us." I was struck by his confession.

"Dan, that's not something you need to worry about. I don't want to lose you, I don't want to make that mistake."

"Neither do I."

"But Dan, we made a vow of total honesty, right?"

"Yes."

"Well I have to admit that I'm curious. I'm curious to know what it's like to have a big dick in me. I want to know what kind of a difference it will make. Not in our fantasies, but in real life."

"You do?"

"Oh God, yes. Dan, I'll be right back."

I went to the bathroom, coming back with a toilet paper roll in my hand.

"Dan, this might be a little embarrassing, but Cheryl said it might help you to understand my needs. She said I should put this toilet paper roll on your cock. If you slip easily inside it, you're too thin to fully please most women. If you don't stick out the other side by a good amount, you're probably not long enough. If you can't do either, then Cheryl says you are definitely incapable of fucking a pussy the way it needs."

I put the paper roll on Dan's cock. It fit easily over his penis. His head didn't quite poke out the other side.

"Wow," was all I could say as I lifted the roll off.

Dan seemed ashamed, but his cock had never been harder.

"Did that make you feel inadequate?" I asked him while I straddled him and teasingly stroked his cock.

"Yes," Dan admitted.

"But did it turn you on, too?"

"Yes!" Dan said as I stroked harder.

"Does it turn you on to know that you're small?"

"Yes!"

"Does it turn you on when you slip your hard dick into me, knowing I can easily handle you?"

"Yes!"

"And does it turn you on to know that I can't come on your dick unless we stroke my clit?"

"Uh!"

"And wouldn't you love to see a big dick inside me, see what it could do to me?"

"Oh yes."

"Well, you're going to get your chance, Dan, do you want that? Do you want a chance?"

"Oh Linda, yes!!"

After Dan came, he worked my pussy with his fingers until I came hard also. But while it was a good come, it didn't really knock me out. I slept fitfully.

CHAPTER 9

DOING WHAT I HAVE TO DO

∽⟊∾

T HE NEXT DAY, A dilemma. Should I hold Dan to his word? Or should I ask him again when he'd had a chance to think about it, when he was not super turned on? Before I could question myself further, I took control.

When Dan got back from work that day, I told him flatly, in a way that took no denial, "We're going to Cheryl's on Friday." He nodded in agreement, without a protest. I felt a quiver inside me.

As the four of us had snacks and drinks around Cheryl's kitchen table that Friday, it was more than a bit awkward. So much had been decided ... but how did you get from one point to the next? Another drink ... and maybe another. I was starting to get cold feet. But then a pipe got passed around. Eventually there was more laughter, less tension. Things got a bit hazy. Eddie grabbed my hand and led me obediently outside. Dan gazed in my direction with an ache in his eyes, but I saw Cheryl touching his arm, pulling him back.

Eddie was wearing floppy cloth pants that would have seemed feminine on most guys, but on Eddie, the concept of feminine was irrelevant. His white V-neck rippled. For a moment, he held my hand and looked me in the eye. I thought he was going to lead me into the hot tub, but he stood closer instead. I felt dizzy with crushed-out feelings, flashbacks to freshman year of high school, stammering out a conversation with Phil, our high school quarterback/prom king.

Losing my nerve was definitely an option; a part of me wanted to go inside. If I'd done so, this story might have ended. But it didn't, because Eddie took my right hand and placed it on his cock. As I felt the shape of it, a surge of sensation rippled through me. It felt so massive, so solid, so … right. I found myself rubbing it, circling my hand around it, feeling it twitch to life. I probably moaned, who knows. Before I could have second thoughts, Eddie grabbed me forcefully and pulled me down. I was almost angry as my knees whacked the deck, but in that same instant, Eddie lowered his pants and his fat cock sprung out and gently slapped me in the face.

I felt like such a slut looking at that dick. I hardly ever sucked Dan's, certainly not from this submissive position. "Suck it," Eddie said as he looked down. I obeyed him mindlessly. I wrapped one hand around his cock and started working the head of that big shaft in my mouth.

Slowly but surely, Eddie's cock began to harden and rise to its full state. I always thought big cocks would droop, but in Eddie's case, it stood straight up, just like last time, angling even higher. As his shaft grew harder, I found myself less and less hesitant. Soon I had two hands on his cock, working them up and down while licking and sucking that head. All I could think about was what *that* would feel like inside me. Eddie lifted me onto the side of their picnic table and forcefully pushed my legs wide open.

"Are you ready for this huge cock?" (He had a hell of a lot of nerve bragging about his cock like that, I thought to myself. But fuck he's right!)

"Oh God, yes!" I called out. I realized that I had no idea where Dan was, and at that moment, I didn't care. I could feel my legs all slippery. Even with almost no foreplay, I was flowing, I was ready. I stared as Eddie slipped a condom on quickly and worked his head into my pussy, forcing his way in with a loud "plop."

"Oh, wow," I said. "It's in."

"Barely," said Eddie.

I was surprised that it didn't hurt more, but then again, I was *really* wet. Eddie slowly started pushing his cock into me, one more inch, then another.

"Umm … Ow!!" That part did hurt.

"Ow?" Eddie said. "Want me to stop?"

"No, keep, uhh, going …" Eddie smiled, a little arrogantly for my taste, and kept pushing.

"Stop!" I said and looked down. About half his cock was inside me, but that was all I could handle. My lips stretched obscenely around his shaft. Actually, it hurt. I felt a wave of relief: Eddie's cock didn't feel good inside me. Dan was all the man I needed.

But then Eddie pulled his cock back, gradually working it, just a few inches in and out, stopping at around five inches where he hit resistance. I wasn't sure what I was feeling, but it wasn't great. It kind of hurt, but it was different from what I was used to.

Without warning Eddie pushed in deeper, harder.

"Ow!!" I called out again. This time he was maybe six inches in … I had been penetrated deeper in the past, maybe, but not as thickly, and it fucking hurt. "Ow!!"

Suddenly Eddie turned gentle on me.

"It's okay," said Eddie in a comforting tone that really startled me. I was expecting him to try to rip me apart, and I would tell him "Enough!" But he tricked me. "We'll take it nice and slow for a bit," he said.

For about five minutes, Eddie just moved in and out. It felt more like an invasive medical exam than a good lay, but the time passed. About five minutes in, I started to feel more of

a warmth, an itchy stretchy feeling. Eddie was moving in and
out a bit faster, and I felt a rhythm building. Before I knew it,
I was coming on his cock. It happened so fast I didn't realize it
was happening.

"I came on your cock, wow!" Not something I was used to.

"No you didn't," said Eddie.

"Oh yes I did," I said in irritation, as he worked his cock
in and out. "I know my orgasms better than you do." I was
annoyed at Eddie's cocky way. What did he know about my
orgasms?

"I'll show you an orgasm!" Eddie said, which made me
laugh. What a tool!

The next thing I knew, Eddie had jammed his entire cock
inside me.

"Ow!!"

"I thought so," he said to me smugly, his cock wedged inside
me. "You've opened up for me."

"Let me show you something," he said. With that, he started
thrusting in and out, not very quickly yet, but deep thrusts, all
the way in. It hurt for a couple more minutes, but then the hurt
went away, and it just felt warm and deep and full.

"Oh Eddie, that feels good," I said, looking up with a bit
more respect.

"Hang on," he said, as he started thrusting a little faster. I
started to realize that the joke was on me, that I was in the hands
of an expert cocksman. Before I knew what was happening,
I felt waves of sensation surging through my body. I pushed
back at him, giving him more pussy to work with.

The cock worship part of the encounter kicked in.

"Oh Eddie, your cock feels good inside me," I blurted.

"Wait ..." Eddie said, "just wait," as he thrust rhythmically
into me. It was like he was massaging my insides, pulling me
out but not violently. A few more minutes of that ...

"Do you want to feel your pussy come?"

"Oh yes," I said helplessly, no longer combative.

"Okay then ...."

With that, Eddie grabbed my ass cheeks and started to really pound me. He was pulling my ass up to him and it was good, it was different, it was an itch getting scratched, an itch I had never known I was walking around with, but here it was, deeper and deeper and I was going to come, I was going to come, I was going to ....

"Come!!" he called out! I had never *ever* had a man command me to come before, much less someone who could make me do it. He told me later that with all the fucking he had done, he could feel the ripples of pre-vaginal orgasms moving up his cock, some kind of seismic sensations warning of the pending ....

"Oh ... my ... god!!"

I was trembling, shaking, lost in sensation. My clit was so happy with his thickness scraping, but that was just the cherry on top. This went so much deeper, so much fuller. I shook and screamed and trembled, and on the other side, I was his.

Before I could say anything else, Eddie scooped me up and held me on his dick as he bounced me up and down. After a cum that deep, a part of me wanted to stop, but another part of me wanted to keep going, keep feeling that sensation, better than my pussy had ever felt, speared on his cock. It was amazing how he could raise me up and drop me, letting my own weight pound on this cock, taking almost all of it, making these sleazy obnoxious plunging sounds. Dan could have never raised me up and lowered me like this. I would have instantly fallen off of him. My lips clung to his thickness on the way out, scraping and grabbing at him in ecstasy. Just a couple minutes of that and my greedy pussy was coming again, so hard, so deep, so out of fucking control: "oh you fucking stud!!" or whatever came out of my mouth—who knows—as I was hit with waves of glorious amoral sensation.

From behind me, I heard cheering. Cheryl walked out on the deck from the living room where they had been watching, holding Dan's hand, bringing the two of them closer. Then she clapped.

"Bravo!" Cheryl said, "What a performance!" She looked over at Dan, but he was shell-shocked. I looked at Dan too, but as a stranger. I was in a sexual daze. I stared compulsively at Eddie. His cock was engorged, hanging in an arrogant, half-hard state, glistening with all my juices.

Pleasure quickly gave way to self-consciousness as I became aware that my sluttiness was on display in front of Dan. Before I knew it, we were dressing and leaving, faking our way through the awkwardness.

Chapter 10

A New Itch

⚭

Y OU MIGHT THINK THAT things went bonkers after that encounter, but that was the strangest part: we settled back into our old routine. I was sore for a few days, not really wanting to have sex, but Dan and I felt a closeness between us, a shyness, and for a couple of weeks after that we made love almost every night. I started to feel a quiet relief; I think he did, too. It was as if we had both gotten something out of our systems, and now we could resume our normal lives.

But a few weeks in, I became aware of an itch inside me, an urge that wasn't getting scratched. I found myself thinking about Eddie. I tried my old routine of masturbating myself to sleep, but that didn't really do it for me. Dan was sweet. He seemed to understand what I was going through, but we didn't really talk about it. Then, one day, Dan left early for a meeting. I realized I was horny, but then I had an even more shattering realization: I was in control of our relationship. *I could do what I wanted.* It was a horrible thought, an awful thought, but a sexy thought as well.

I found myself calling Cheryl, and within a couple hours I was sitting in her living room.

"I know why you're here," she said to me, smiling in that all-knowing way.

"Why?" I said self-consciously, embarrassed that I was so obvious.

"You need to get fucked again."

I was silent, embarrassed.

"You wish Eddie was here because you need to get fucked so badly."

I started to feel squirmy and awkward in front of my friend.

"Well, here's the deal. You can be with Eddie one more time, but that's it. And then you have to level with your husband."

"About what?" I asked, fearing what she would say.

"That you have needs he can't fulfill. And that you have a right to get them filled."

I paused, not really knowing what to say.

"Linda, your marriage is in trouble. But you can fix it."

"Dan and I are fine."

"But you won't be ... now that you've been corrupted," Cheryl said with sexy authority.

"Things might go back to normal for a little bit, but in the back of your mind, something has changed. And at some point, something's gonna happen, hot guys are gonna hit on you, and you're going to cheat on Dan, and that's going to change things between you."

More silence ... I didn't know if Cheryl was right or not, but I knew she was making me horny.

"Dan is a great husband, but he's not your sexual equal."

I didn't even know what that meant. Something about it made me mad, mad at her, mad at her for disrespecting Dan like that. But I was here ... distracted by a constant pull. Whether that pull was a primal need or a weakness of character, I didn't know. But I was here.

"Well, Eddie will be home soon ..." Cheryl said. "Why don't we get into the hot tub and wait for him there?"

Looking at Cheryl's rippling, muscular body didn't help my

horniness, which went up a notch as she tossed her towel aside and lowered herself in.

"I always feel so flabby around you," I told her as I took off my shorts.

"Oh girl, you have no idea!" Cheryl said to me. "I love the curve of your hips, the way your tits sway. You're perfect!"

I had never felt perfect, but I did like her staring at me.

When Eddie walked out, he seemed completely unsurprised that I was back.

"Baby, I need you to fuck my girl again," Cheryl told him.

"No problem, honey," Eddie said, a little too arrogantly for my taste. But then his shorts were down and that big cock was swinging again. I had to have it inside me.

Eddie teased me more than the last time. He ate my pussy out slowly, more expertly than I would have liked. I was hoping I could give top pussy eating honors to Dan. But Eddie's tongue knew its way around a pussy pretty well. He knew just when to tug on my clit and how much pressure to apply. Dan understood my emotions better, but Eddie had technical skills.

By the time he bent me over the picnic table and put his cock inside me, I was so drippy and cummy I knew I was going to spew all over him.

"Oh Eddie! That feels so good!"

The feeling of his cock stretching my pussy was amazing. As much as I hated to admit it, the sensation was foreign. Not possible with Dan. With effort, my pussy could grip Dan's cock, but Eddie's expanded and filled my pussy. No concentration needed, just letting go, giving into the sensations. The feeling was incredible—in that slutty moment, it was worth my marriage, my friendship with Cheryl, anything.

But it wasn't just the sensations, it was the intensity of submitting to Eddie, being utterly conquered after walking around in control all day long. But I wasn't in control now! I needed to come so badly. I wanted Eddie to fuck me right up to my uterus, to fill my pussy with his seed, to make me his slut, to impregnate me without regard to the consequences.

Eddie turned me over on the picnic table, and I put my ass in the air, searching for him. He was slapping his cock on my ass, making wet smacking sounds all over, while I waited for him to enter.

"Baby, don't put it back in her yet," I heard Cheryl say to me.

"Oh, why not?" I called out, pushing my ass out, reaching for his cock.

"Because I want you to admit it," Cheryl said.

"What??" I called out.

"That Eddie fucks you better than Dan does."

"Oh, why??"

"Because I said so."

I felt irritated at Cheryl, annoyed that she was stopping Eddie from fucking me. That itch I had felt for two weeks was so strong, I couldn't think of anything but scratching it. I gave in.

"Yeah, Eddie fucks me so good, so much better than Dan. Eddie, please fuck me, please!"

Without saying a word, Eddie slipped his cock inside me and started moving inside. Oh … that itch was getting scratched now! As he pounded, it was getting scratched more, and soon it was ecstasy and he was pounding me and I was cheating on Dan and it felt so slutty and so right and I was going to keep fucking Eddie no matter what ….

Coming all over Eddie's cock was amazing, I even felt some fluid pushing out—another first—literally all over his cock, leaking all over the picnic table. It was everything I needed. But then it was over.

CHAPTER 11

BAD GIRLS UNDERSTAND BETA BOYS

❦

BACK INSIDE, CHERYL AND I drank lemonade. I was already feeling pretty bad, though not for the reasons I expected. I didn't feel bad about cheating on Dan, but I did feel strange about having sex with Cheryl's boyfriend—even with her obvious approval. As for Dan, I did wonder how my marriage could survive this last encounter, and I wasn't sure I liked the slut who was coming out now.

"Cheryl, I'm sorry. I don't know what came over me."

"Linda, there's no need to apologize. You've been getting a substandard fucking—that makes you a little famished for a real cock inside you."

I hated the way Cheryl was talking, especially about Dan, but it really turned me on too.

"But lots of couples don't have perfect sex lives," I said defensively.

"That may be true," said Cheryl. "But you're a beautiful woman in your sexual prime, and what this male-run society doesn't want to accept is that you have sexual control right now. You get to have whatever you want."

"I don't want to lose Dan!"

"Oh, you don't have to lose Dan, you don't have to lose him at all," said Cheryl. "He knows deep down he can't totally please you. Remember what I told you?

"What?"

"It turns him on."

I blushed a little thinking about it.

"Did you see him when you were fucking Eddie the first time?" Cheryl asked me.

"Well, I wasn't paying a lot of attention," I said, and we both laughed.

"Well, we were standing at the window, looking out on the deck. His little cock was really hard. He got rock hard in my hand when I teased him about his size and told him how much better Eddie was pleasing you."

I didn't know what to say.

"He couldn't get enough of watching you," Cheryl went on. "Little guys like Dan want—and need—to know their sexual place."

"I find that hard to believe," I said to Cheryl, trying to sound convincing. "Dan doesn't like to feel inferior, especially to someone he doesn't respect all that much."

"Well, that's a bit of a trick," Cheryl said. "Dan thinks he is a better man than Eddie, and he's probably right about that—except in one way, one really important way, and knowing that drives him absolutely crazy."

My world had been turned upside down. How would I ever get it right?

"But you don't have it figured out either," I said to Cheryl, going on the offensive.

"How's that?"

"Well, Eddie doesn't satisfy you emotionally, I know that."

"No, that's true," Cheryl said. "I won't stay with him forever ... but, I'm getting my brains fucked out every night, and that's not so bad, is it?" She looked at me teasingly; I couldn't help but resent her a little bit. "And I have some girlfriends I love dearly who give me plenty of emotional support along the way.

"It's hard to find everything you want in one man," Cheryl continued. "Women usually settle for domestic love, that stable 'good provider' love that guys like Dan give. But they lose out on the sexual side, which is why you were over here on your hands and knees today, sticking your ass out for Eddie's stud cock, cheating on your husband and risking your whole marriage just to come like you needed to."

I fell into reflection.

"Women have had a raw deal for a long time," Cheryl said. "Now that we finally have more sexual power, we still don't know what we want or how to get what we're looking for. And if we insist on the importance of size to sexual pleasure, we sound like shallow sluts.

"I do know this, though," Cheryl went on. "Emotional love is not enough for a sexually empowered woman. Most women crave those deep, baby-making orgasms that only a guy like Eddie can give. And it's not just about selfish pleasure either. It's about biological certainty, the deep drive to mate with alpha males to continue our species. It's a powerful force … but you know that now," she said, smiling wickedly.

I wasn't amused. I started to feel despair, knowing she was right, but somehow feeling she was wrong, too. And wondering what to do about it either way.

"You know what's interesting about guys like Dan?" Cheryl asked.

"No," I said.

"Well, there's two things that turn them on the most. One is seeing their girl get satisfied by a real man like Eddie. The second is getting teased by a hot girl like me that would never fuck them."

"I don't understand."

"Well, most guys are too jealous and insecure to let a girl like you get their needs met. Dan, on the other hand, loves you and wants you to be happy. That takes a lot of strength, a lot of maturity …. Most guys wouldn't have the guts. But he still needs to be put in his place a little bit. That allows him to embrace his sexual role in your marriage."

I was still confused.

"While you were riding Eddie and coming all over him, I was stroking Dan's cock. You know what I was saying to him?" Cheryl smiled wickedly.

"What?"

"I was letting him know that he was lucky to have a hot girl like you, that I would *never* fuck him."

"You said that?"

"Yeah, and he asked me to say it to him again, and I was happy to tell him that his little penis was way too small to please my demanding pussy. He squirted like a charm. All the beta boys do."

"Beta boys?"

"Guys who have a submissive side, usually because they realize deep down they aren't quite adequate."

I was mad at Cheryl for giving this so much thought. Usually I could win an argument with her, but she had really thought through this.

"Yeah, I whispered in his ear that he was lucky to have a beautiful girl like you, that I would never fuck a thin little cock like his, and I rubbed my pussy against his leg to show him how near, yet how far, my juicy pussy was from his little ineffective dick, and just like a charm, he squirted all over my hand—right away. He couldn't stop himself."

"Cheryl!" I called out, mad but excited by her total dominance of Dan.

"Meanwhile, while Dan is squirting helplessly in my hand, Eddie is getting all that intense, gripping stimulation from your pussy, and yet he is fucking you relentlessly, not coming, fucking you in front of your horny husband, who can't get enough of my fingers wrapped around his tiny penis and my wet pussy on his thigh. Actually, I don't blame Dan for coming so fast—little guys like him get *way* more friction from hand jobs than they do inside a real pussy."

I found myself laughing and hating myself for it. Damn her.

"Sure enough, Dan got hard again watching you fuck, and when I asked him if he liked watching you get filled up like he was unable to do, he was right on the edge again."

I was speechless.

"Then I asked him if he liked knowing how inadequate he was, if he liked that I knew his little secret, that he was a man with a little boy's cock that couldn't please his wife, and guess what?"

"What?" I asked.

"His little dick squirted all over my hand again!"

I wanted to smack her, but she was making me wet, too!

"And Linda, face it, if you didn't love Dan—if you were just looking for a one-night stand at a bar, you wouldn't fuck him, either."

I felt really slutty when she said that.

"No, you'd fuck Eddie ten times out of ten in that situation. Dan gets his sexual power from your emotional connection, with a bond of sexual attraction from when you first fell in love. But once that initial attraction fades—that's when the cravings begin."

She was right, more right than I wanted her to be. How come I never heard talk like this on *Oprah*? All the reassuring things you hear about relationships, and here came this damning but scarily accurate view of the sexual dilemmas women face.

"So what do I do?" I asked her.

"Well, the thing is, you don't want to lose Dan," Cheryl said. It was not what I was expecting her to say. "Let's face it, guys like Dan are hard to find; he's marriage material, and if you lose him, you're gonna regret it. He loves you enough to humble himself in front of you, and that take a lot of guts. Plus, he's a great husband and provider besides.

"On the other hand, you have a problem," Cheryl continued.

"Because your sex life flatlined, and after Eddie, you're a sexual time bomb …. So you have to be honest. Totally honest."

"Yeah?"

"Sexual connection starts with lust, but once you go long term, it's about honesty."

"Jeez, you sound like a therapist!" I said.

"Well, I am a volunteer counselor, you know that right? Anyhow, you have to tell him all about your fantasies, and get him to share his. From there, anything goes! But you have to do it together."

"Yeah, we started doing that," I said.

"And yet, you didn't take it all the way," said Cheryl, "because you're here, and he's not. You have to claim your needs *inside* the relationship and see if he is ready to meet you halfway. From what I can see, he is."

I fell silent again. I had underestimated Cheryl, viewing her as a caution-to-the-wind hippie chick. That was still true. But there was more. It was like Cheryl understood my body, my conflicting needs, better than I did. Just like last time, I had a sudden urge to leave, to get out of that house and go back to whatever life I was trying to lead before, unspoiled by these experiences.

CHAPTER 12

SINS OF SUMMER

∞

A ND SO I LEFT. And I managed to forget. I put Cheryl and
Eddie out of my head. I thought I would be so consumed
by guilt that I would not be able to be around Dan without
breaking down, but for whatever reason, that wasn't the case.
I didn't want to make a habit of cheating on Dan, but the guilt
was nowhere to be found. In some odd way, I felt defiant and
justified.

It wasn't even a week before I had an incident. It was an
incident in my own head.

It happened at an odd time. I found myself looking up at
Dan, watching as he pounded his cock into me. It dawned on
me that my pussy was somewhat indifferent to what he was
doing. It felt good, yes, but my pussy remembered something
much more intense. *Dan is not your sexual equal.* What were
the implications of that taboo thought? Can you be married to
someone who is not your sexual equal?

I probably could have found a way to sedate these thoughts,
but change came along, this time in the form of a vacation.
Dan's division at work met a big milestone. Dan, as the project
manager, was given two week's vacation in the islands. We were

off to an island called Turks and Caicos—a place recommended to Dan by his colleagues.

We went in the summer, which is a hot time of year to visit, but we both needed to get away. I'm someone who likes the heat. The first week of our trip was spent largely in our own hotel room. We didn't go out much, had some lovely talks, some tender but unspectacular sex, and plenty of room service. We also walked along the beach. One day, we decided to walk a bit longer. Eventually, the beach reached a point where it was blocked by a broken down peer. Someone had stacked a pile of rocks and hotel construction signs. You had to venture into the woods to walk around it, but we were feeling adventurous.

On the other side was a sign: "nude beach: dress at your own discretion." I smiled at Dan and we kept walking. There weren't a lot of people on the beach, but one thing's for sure: they were all butt naked. A few elderly couples, skin dried from years of sunny living, waved friendly greetings from their lounge chairs.

I obeyed the urge to get naked. It felt good to have the sun on my breasts. I put my bikini in my bag. Dan seemed shy.

"It's okay," I told him. "No one cares here. Try it—it feels good."

Dan took off his trunks and we kept walking, holding hands. Three college-age guys walked by, beer bottles in hand. When they got close, they took a hard look at me. I felt a tingling sensation between my legs, knowing I had their attention, knowing I still had that golden hip power, despite being a good fifteen years older than they were. My breasts, not as aggressively perky as they had once been, still arrested the male gaze. *You have your pick of these men.* I found myself glancing at their crotches as they walked by. They looked a lot like Dan down there, though one was definitely floppier and … uncircumcised. I looked at him the longest, trying not to stare.

After we passed them, I turned to Dan and said something

I wasn't expecting to say: "See, honey, you don't have anything to worry about."

My frankness prompted a new look on Dan's face, one I would eventually come to recognize: surprise hiding some embarrassment and a flash of lust.

But I had spoken too soon. The next two guys who walked by were older. Both wore straw hats but were totally naked otherwise. They had the flabby bellies of businessmen. I found myself smiling at them and sneaking glances downward. One of them had a tiny button of a dick, shriveled and shy. The other had a big soft cock. It was long and thin, dangling back and forth between his legs. I felt a primal tingle and stared at it too long. The man seemed to wink as I passed, both of them getting an eyeful of my tits.

I was starting to feel very powerful. It was odd—here I was with my husband, yet I felt like the queen of the beach.

"What a contrast in cocks!" I exclaimed to Dan. He laughed but seemed kind of shy about it, like he wanted to change the subject, like he wanted to be somewhere else.

"Let's lie down for a bit," I said. "I want to get some tan on my boobs." We made our way toward the edge of the beach, leading into the woods. Dan loosened up a bit, more so when I asked him to rub lotion on my breasts. But then he started to get an erection, and I told him to get off me. "I don't think we're supposed to have sexy time at the nude beach," I snapped.

Naptime. Dan read his book, John Steinbeck from the airport classics rack. I slept. I turned over from time to time, worried I would get a sunburn on my back. While I had napped, it had gotten late. The sun was still out, but it was on the downward slope. The nude beachers had left—tourists tended to be early risers here, looking to get on fishing boats and snorkeling trips.

"Excuse me, do you have the time?" a booming voice startled me.

I looked up from my nap to see a big smiling man, a black man, his skin as dark as most locals. He was not your typical island boat worker—younger guys who were in good shape from working on fishing boats. He had a pretty big belly, an older guy's body, but I forgot about his belly as soon as my eyes took in his cock. Almost half erect, it hung down obscenely, protruding like a big fat snake. I couldn't believe this man was willing to stand in front of me with a half-erection, obviously inspired by my own nudity. It was the most monstrous cock I had ever seen. It wasn't beautiful, but it commanded attention. The weirdest thing: he was wearing a fanny pack around his waist. No other clothes. He looked distracting, ridiculous.

I dug for my watch, buried in my beach bag, knowing Dan had forgotten his.

"It's uh ... six o'clock," I stammered.

"Thank you!" The man boomed out, louder than necessary. "My better half expects me home at nine o'clock. I have three hours to get her to give me three more hours," he chuckled, a dumb joke that made me smile somehow. He had a disarming way about him. His tone was better than his material.

"I'm sorry; it was rude of me not to introduce myself. I am Benedict. My friends call me Benny."

Benny reached down, shook Dan's hand. Then he came over, shook my hand. It seemed as if he made an effort to get nearer than he needed to. His dick was close enough to whack me in the face. I stared compulsively at his massive penis, but at the same time, I was annoyed at Benny and wanted him to leave.

"Well, I guess I should be going," Benny said, and started to walk away from us. Once he started to go, I wished he hadn't.

"Benny, sure you don't want to hang out for a while?" I called out to him. "After all, you have three hours to kill."

Benny chuckled ....

"We could use some tips from a local, too!" I called out. Benny turned and walked back toward us, his cock swaying all around.

Benny borrowed a towel, took off his fanny pack, and lay down.

"I'm surrounded by men," I said to ease the tension, but it was surprisingly natural lying between them.

We all laughed about Benny's fanny pack and how funny it looked on a man when that was the only thing he was wearing. Then we made small talk about the island; Benny told us the fun spots we should check out. During the small talk, I savored the moment. Something was about to happen. My pussy was throbbing like crazy, getting wetter by the minute. And I was going to make it happen.

"Benny, I couldn't help but notice ... you have a really magnificent penis."

"Oh thank you," Benny said. "I do get a lot of compliments ... would you ... like to touch it? I mean, if it's okay with Dan."

Benny and I both laughed when he said that. What Dan wanted didn't seem relevant.

"Yes I would."

With that, I reached over and grabbed his penis with my right hand.

"Wow, Benny ... it feels so thick and meaty."

"That's it, Linda," Benny encouraged me. "I like how you work it."

"Benny, look how big it's getting."

Benny's cock continued to swell to life in my hand. It was still bent, but getting harder.

"It's already much bigger than Dan's, and it's not nearly hard yet," I said admiringly.

Benny laughed, enjoying his moment.

With that, I got up and moved to the other side of Benny.

"I want Dan to get a better view of this, Benny," I said. "As you can see, Dan has a small penis, so he doesn't know what it's like to get stroked like this, and I want him to see." Benny chuckled; he seemed to understand this sexual dynamic. I placed both hands on Benny's cock and worked it. Even with both hands, his head stuck way out the top of them.

I could see Dan stroking his cock in the background, he

was already rock hard, almost in a daze from the shock and pleasure of what was happening. Seeing Dan like that gave me the confidence to take it further.

"Benny, what a beauty. You must have fucked a lot of tourist pussies with this," I said, getting wet just thinking about it.

"I guess I've had my share," Benny said casually.

"You've probably wrecked a lot of marriages," I said to Benny as I stroked him.

"I don't know about that," said Benny.

"Benny, can I ask you something?"

"Sure Linda, as long as you don't stop stroking. That feels fantastic!"

"Have you ever fucked a girl in front of her boyfriend?"

"Funny you should ask that, Linda," Benny said. "I used to avoid those kind of scenes, but in the last few years, I've realized how popular it can be."

"That's good," I said while I was stroking him. "Because I want you to fuck me in front of Dan."

"Really?" asked Benny. I felt his cock hardening as I straddled him to jack him off.

"Yes. Dan's penis can't fill me up and I want to show him how good a big man like you can make my pussy feel. He needs to see it so he can squirt and watch me come hard! Isn't that right, Dan?"

Benny's cock was now as hard as I figured a bloated monster like that could get, and Dan was jerking off feverishly—I saw him coming in hard fast spurts.

"Oh Dan, you squirted already?" I looked over and asked.

Dan smiled sheepishly.

"Your little cock loves seeing me like this; you can't help but come fast. But Benny, he's not coming at all, is he? Not at all!"

It was true, Benny wasn't anywhere close to coming, but he was hard as he could get now, jutting up with a small bent toward his stomach.

"Jeez Benny, how big is that cock?"

"Well, it's been measured as big as eleven inches, but to be honest with you, I think it's more like ten," Benny said, as if apologizing.

"Well, it's plenty damn big," I said.

"Guys, can you both stand up for me?" I asked them, looking around to see if anyone was watching. But the beach was deserted.

They both stood up, obeying me.

"Now stand next to each other."

They moved closer together.

"Closer ..." I said, moving them together with my arms.

"Wow," I said.

"I was going to have a cock contest, but there's not much of a contest, is there?"

Benny laughed loudly, with a touch of cruelty—and so did I.

It was pretty shocking to see the comparison. Dan's cock was all shriveled up from coming hard, tiny and withdrawn. Benny's cock stood almost straight out, bending from the weight of itself, ten thick inches from his body. It was as if they were different genders.

"Dan, this isn't fair, let's at least get your tiny penis hard," I said to him. That was the first time I had ever called Dan "tiny"; he twitched right to life as I said it, clearly liking the truth of my words.

I stroked Benny's shaft absently with my left hand, while working on Dan's with my right. I felt it grow in my fingers.

"Oh there it is!" I said. "Let's get this cock hard!"

Dan moaned and twitched in my hands. I was dripping quite a bit myself.

Dan's cock twitched to life ... getting harder by the second. Soon it was stiff, slippery with his previous come.

"Oh Dan, there you are! But look how much smaller you are! See that?"

Dan said, "Yes." How could he not? But he was moaning, too.

"Dan, be honest with me. Do you like my body?"

"Yes."

"Is it hot?" As I asked him that, I swayed my hips around so he could have a good look at me.

"Oh God, yes."

"Do I look like I deserve to have my pussy fucked—fucked real good?"

"Oh, yes!!"

"And Dan, I want you to be honest, which cock do you think is made for filling up a beautiful pussy like mine?"

"His."

"Do you want to see him fuck me, Dan?"

"Oh Yes!!"

"Do you want to see him give me what you can't, what I need so badly?"

"God, yes!" With that, Dan came again in my hand, not so much come this time.

"Wow Dan that was fast—doesn't take you long," I said as I stared intently at Benny's near-hard cock, nowhere near coming yet, despite my constant stroking.

"Okay, Dan, I'm going to show you how I get what I need."

Benny laughed, and I did a little, too. It was just so clear that Dan was outmatched. Clearly it turned Benny on, just as it did me.

"Good thing Benny's cock is still hard and ready to fuck a pussy."

With that, I started jacking Benny off with both hands, licking the head.

Between licks I said, "Look at this two–hander, Dan! It is so intense to jack a cock with two hands like this, getting him ready for me. I can jack you off with two fingers, but not Benny!" I couldn't believe how mean I was being, but in some strange way, I also felt justified.

"Oh, but there's a problem," I said. "I don't have any condoms."

"That's okay," Benny said, "I've got you covered there."

Without notice, Benny pushed me back on the towel, a little bit roughly. Dan looked my way protectively. Benny stood up tall, took off his fanny pack, unzipped it, took out a condom. He rolled it over his huge cock, making it seem that much more engorged. The condom only fit over about two thirds of it, which was so erotic for me to see. I'd never seen a condom that didn't slide easily on Dan's cock. I masturbated while Benny put the condom on, spreading my legs wantonly.

Then he was kneeling, placing that big cockhead up against my lips.

"Don't hurt me!" I cried out.

"Oh, don't worry baby, we'll take it nice and slow," he said with a comforting but cocky smile.

He really knows what he's doing, I thought to myself. Then I saw his big cockhead, or heard his big cockhead, plunk inside me. It was a mixture of pleasure and pain, a jolting sensation.

"Ow!" I called out. He just left his cockhead in there for a minute, letting me get used to the feel of it. I saw the rest of his cock still outside my legs. I spread wider, wondering how he was going to fit that fatness inside me.

"That's right, you're nice and wet for me," he said as he pushed his cock a couple more inches inside.

"Oh!" was all I could say to that. I felt totally stuffed, a bit uncomfortable. He pressed a little deeper, about five inches of his thick cock inside me. He was as far back as Dan can get, but it felt way different, and just like with Eddie the first time, it didn't feel all that good. I was half-hoping it would feel really bad from here on out, then I could somehow get this sluttiness out of my head, go back to being a loyal wife.

"That's all for now," he said, a good half of his cock still outside me. "Time to work what we have in there …."

So he started, pulling his cock out just a couple of inches, then pushing it back inside me. It still hurt quite a bit, and I found myself biting my lip, bracing as he took his slow, steady strokes. I was up on my elbows, taking a careful look at my pussy under this assault. A couple more minutes of thrusting, and it *did* start to feel good.

"That feels nice ..." I said with my arms wrapped around him.

"We're just getting warmed up," he said reassuringly. "Now are you ready for some real fucking?"

"Oh please ..." I said kind of helplessly, between a yes and a no.

With that, he pressed my legs nice and wide and gave his cock a push!

"Ahhh!" I cried out. Propped up on elbows again, I could see that a good portion of his cock was inside me.

"That's it," he said, "That's it."

"Don't push any more inside me; that's all I can take!!" I pleaded with him.

"No problem," Benny said, "Don't you worry, I won't go any deeper than this ...."

And with that, he started stroking in and out, withdrawing a few inches then slowly pressing them back in, about seven inches inside me. In, and out, in, and out. My body was consumed by the sensations. But then he started picking up the pace. As he promised, Benny went no farther in. He withdrew all but the head and pushed it back inside me.

"Ugh" was maybe what I said then. This was a different type of experience; I didn't have the language for it yet.

He started pounding me pretty good. I could feel his thickness dragging against my clit, pulling my pussy lips in and out, coating his cock with my juice. His belly flopped as he moved in and out of me, faster and faster.

I could feel a strange itchy hot sensation building between my legs—and in just a few more thrusts, that itchy hotness was spreading up my body and I was wrapping my legs around his and calling out, "I'm coming!! Oh fuck I'm coming!!" Wave after wave of orgasms bucked through my body.

All he could do was laugh, loving his effect on me. I was

amazed, annoyed. I had never felt anything like it .... It was like Eddie times two.

I could see the beads of sweat along my belly and thighs, his cock still deep inside me.

"Wow ..." I said as he kept his cock still inside me.

"That felt good, didn't it baby?"

"Yeah!" I said helplessly.

"Want to feel even better?"

"I'm not sure I can ...."

"Oh, you can .... I just have to break you in a little more ...."

I was starting to get sore, but I wasn't done as long as Benny wasn't ... and with that, he started thrusting in and out again, slowly.

"That was ... amazing ..." was all I could say.

"Yeah, you needed to come like that. I love helping women come ... especially when their husbands can't help them in that way ...." He said it in a kind way, but for some reason I laughed a little bit ... then I remembered, for the first time in a while, that Dan was still there.

I could see that Dan had already come, at some point, while I was getting fucked. His half-hard dick was resting on his leg. I returned my attention to Benny.

"Do you want to come even harder?" Benny asked as he started thrusting in and out.

"Oh please ...." I said.

Just like that he was upon me, pushing his body down, raising my ass up, pushing in farther and "Ohhhh!! Dammit!!" I shrieked. He was laying into me now, pounding me so hard I could barely concentrate. My pussy was making obscene sloshing noises as he rammed into me, but I was far from caring. All I could feel was this well of sensation getting stronger and stronger between my legs. I was vaguely aware that he still wasn't all the way inside me.

"That's it baby, now you're really gonna come for me ...."

"Oh!!!" I yelled out, babbling and screaming, pushing my

hips up at him wildly, going after as much cock as I could get, as much as I had ever had.

"Show your husband what a slut you are for me! Show him how hard you can come!"

God what a bastard he was, talking to me like that! I didn't feel like coming, coming would be a betrayal of my husband's abilities, but Benny was pounding and pounding and my pussy was helpless not to respond .... I was thrusting like crazy, sweat and lust and juices everywhere, losing myself in being completely stretched ....

"Oh God I'm coming!!" I screamed, loud enough to carry over the breaking waves. That huge sensation in my pussy burst through my body. Benny pushed my legs wide as I spasmed all over his cock, trembling and shaking while he held me down strong. Then something unexpected happened: I began spurting fluid everywhere, expelling his cock with force as juices gushed out of me. I saw stars; it felt like I passed out and then I was back, back, at sexual peace.

When Benny pulled his cock out, my pussy made loud puffy noises, like a balloon letting out air. It sounded kind of funny; we both laughed. Sweaty and a little spent, Benny lay down beside me. I was sprawled between my husband and Benny again. The situation was surreal. Here I was on this beach, doing something I never would have done in public at home, but here in a foreign country, nothing was the same. The sun was beginning to set, but anyone walking down that beach could have seen us—the wife, the cuckolded husband, and her lover. And I didn't care.

CHAPTER 13

THE EROTICS OF DOMINANCE AND SUBMISSION

⌒

"Wow ... MY PUSSY has never done anything like that before," I marveled. My towel was so wet it was almost gross.

"Yeah, you squirted all over me—it takes a very happy pussy to squirt like that."

"God I have never .... Anyhow ... thanks," I found myself saying to Benny, as if he had just given me a huge drink of water when I was parched. He just laughed, his cock still dangling, swollen against his leg, the condom still half on. That's when I felt guilty, but in a sexual way. "Oh no ... I didn't make you come yet."

"That's all right, baby; there's plenty of time for that," he said. His manner was both arrogant and relaxed, the birthright of men with his gift. I put one hand on his dick and stroked it absentmindedly, marveling at its thickness as I pulled off the condom. That made me think of my husband.

I turned and looked at Dan. "Did you come, honey?"

"Yes," he said sheepishly. Dan's cock was soft and shiny from his come.

As I lay between them, I stroked Dan's cock with my left

land, Benny's with my right. Even though Dan's cock had already come two times, it twitched to life in my hand.

"I can't believe you haven't come yet," I said to Benny. "This one came just from watching." I pointed at Dan's dick. "And he had already come when I was stroking both of you! Meanwhile, Benny, you were servicing the hell out of my little pussy, filling her like she's never been filled, and you haven't come at all."

"Ah, that's okay," said Benny. "This cock has fucked a lot of pussies. It's not easy to make it come."

I had never heard a man talk like that before—yeah, maybe some hollow bragging at parties—but nothing like this, a guy who could back it all up. He said it so matter-of-factly. I felt more tingling between my legs as I continued to stroke both cocks.

"Don't feel bad Dan," said Benny. "I've outlasted a lot of men in my day."

I couldn't help smiling at that, embarrassed but thrilled by his tone.

"I don't know why," Benny said, "but little cocks have a tendency to come much faster than big ones like mine."

"Yeah, we already saw that, didn't we honey?" I said to Dan, teasing him.

I thought I saw a flash of anger on Dan's face, but then came the submission, the moan of pleasure as I stroked him.

"Benny, God, I love your cock," I said to him, letting go of Dan's cock so I could stroke his harder. "Let me see you spurt. Let me see it!"

Before long, I was kneeling, my back to Dan, determined to make Benny cut loose. "C'mon Benny, come! Come!" I stroked him fast as I could with my hand. "Let me see that big dick come!"

My hand released Dan's cock as I started stroking Benny's harder, determined to make it come. It was huge, engorged …. My hand could barely fit around it. My pussy was dripping ….

I knelt on the other side, so Dan could get a good view. "Can you see this good, honey?"

"Ohh … yeah," Dan said as he stroked himself, lost in lust. Benny and I laughed at that.

I started stroking Benny up and down, using two hands to really work his shaft.

"Benny, that is one hell of a cock," I said admiringly.

"Thank you sweetie," he said almost patronizingly.

"Oh God, yes," I said, "I want to see it squirt."

With that, I started rubbing his big balls with one hand while stroking him with the other. I marveled at the size of his balls, not quite the size of tennis balls, but they certainly matched the rest of him. They felt huge, swollen, ready to burst.

"Wow your balls are so much bigger than Dan's," I said, smiling and marveling as I rubbed his balls with one hand while stroking with another. It was so different from jacking off Dan, who was so easily serviced with one hand. Benny deserved both my hands. Hell, he had enough cock for two women. Benny's cock twitched in a strong way. Maybe I was finally getting to him!

"Stroke me faster, baby," Benny said. I never really liked it when men called me "baby," but in his case, it felt right. He deserved to call me whatever he wanted. With obedience and lust, I went back to the two-handed stroking.

"Faster, that's it," Benny said. I upped the tempo again.

"Oh Benny …" I said helplessly. "You are such a fucking stud. Let me see that studcock come. Come for me, Benny!!"

I was stroking him frantically now, shocked at the amount of friction his stud cock could withstand, frustrated that I was having trouble getting an orgasm out of him. But then he came.

Dan usually spurted a couple of super quick and fast bursts, a couple of feet at most; then he was done, just as quickly. Benny didn't spurt high or fast, but he spurted thick shots, one after another. I kept stroking, and he kept spurting. I lost count around eight, with Benny moaning on each ejaculation. A couple more ropey spurts, and he was done. Come was everywhere. There was a huge pool of it around his belly dripping into the sand.

"Oh, wow, Benny!"

He chuckled. "Haven't seen a dick like this come before, huh?"

"Hardly!" I said. "That's incredible. God you are such a man!" I spoke lustfully, not caring about Dan's feelings. Not caring at all. Cleaning up was a bit awkward. We were all conscious of the strangeness of the situation. I used our extra towel to clean Benny up, and I needed pretty much the whole towel to do it.

Eventually, we all began to relax and even doze off. It started to feel natural again, just the three of us, talking openly about life on the island. Dan's erection went away; Benny was calm and floppy. I thought maybe the sex was over, but after about fifteen minutes, listening to Benny talk about restaurants, I had an image of Benny fucking a waitress over the counter, then another of a husband coming back from golf to find his wife riding Benny's cock, her clothes still on, her skirt hiked up, not stopping, just screaming. My pussy twitched.

As if on cue, Benny said, "It was so nice to be able to help you out Linda …."

"What do you mean Benny," I asked, curious what else he might say in front of Dan.

"Well, I could tell you haven't come like that in a while, and your pussy really needed it," Benny said.

I felt embarrassed, but his openness was the ultimate turn-on.

"Oh yeah," I said to Benny. "I needed that bad!"

"You had that look," smiled Benny. "I get that look a lot."

"You mean," I said, "down at the beach?" I smiled back. I thought I saw his cock twitch in the twilight.

"Yes," said Benny. "You had that hungry look about you, your pussy being so deprived …."

"So, Benny, how many … women have you 'helped'?"

"Well," said Benny. "I used to make a point of only being with single girls. But there are so many *fine* married women." He smiled at me and Dan, who smiled back reflexively. Dan seemed to be in some kind of emasculated daze, but all the signs indicated that he was enjoying himself.

"At first, I would do it without the husband's knowledge or permission," said Benny. "But I rarely do that anymore. You see, it never felt right, and besides, I didn't have to. Because so many husbands were asking me to ... help them out."

"Really?" I asked.

"Yes," he said. "Of course, women kept asking, too, but I started telling them: 'I think you would have fewer regrets if your husband or boyfriend agrees, and he can watch if he likes.'"

"And how did that go?" I asked. Dan seemed interested. He also looked like he wanted to be anywhere but here.

"Ups and downs," Benny continued. "Some were shocked and said 'no way!' But I knew it was better if the boyfriend or husband watched ... I found out that if I was firm on this point, many women would take me up on it. They basically needed it bad enough to agree to my terms."

My pussy tingled. No, "need" was not too strong a word.

"Once I tried it this way, I realized how much better it was," said Benny. "It did less damage to their relationships, and often seemed to improve them."

"How?" I asked.

"Well," said Benny, propping himself on his elbows and smiling at me, clearly enjoying our conversation, "the women found it useful for the men to see, the ... difference in sexual satisfaction they were experiencing with me. This changed the feeling between them. Instead of seeing the wife as a cheater and a slut, the men realized that it was not their fault, that their women needed ...."

"More than they could give?" I said, taking a look at Dan's tiny cock, hard as a rock again, but still much smaller than Benny's semi-hard floppy one. I laughed in spite of myself.

This was the heart of the cruel/kind paradox I would come to know as "cuckolding."

"Yes," said Benny. I found my hands moving between my legs, tweaked as I was by this conversation. "In some cases," Benny said, "a whole lot more."

I felt that tingle again while looking at Benny's massive engorged half-hard cock—easily seven thick ropy inches, way bigger than Dan's ever is when hard. Yes, that would explain the enormous difference in the sensations within me.

It was getting dark, and there were a few mosquitoes, but not as many as usual. Benny's big penis snaked down his thigh, illuminated by the setting sun. I reached over and started fondling it again as I talked with him, feeling it flop and twitch, sticky in my hands.

"One other thing changed," said Benny.

"What's that?" I asked, while stroking him with my right hand. My juices were still sticky on his penis, which made me feel a little nasty.

"I started recognizing 'the look,'" Benny said. "These days, when I get that look from a sexy woman with a poorly endowed partner, I don't wait for them to approach me. I approach them to offer my help. Of course, in your case, you did most of the asking."

He made it sound so clinical, but that also made me wet.

"So Benny, how many times have you done this?" I persisted.

"You mean, pleasured a woman with her husband or boyfriend watching?"

"Yes," I said, one hand between my legs and one on his cock, not sure why this conversation was turning me on so much.

"Oh, I don't keep count," Benny said casually.

"Oh yes you do!" I said accusingly, positioning his cock straight in the air, amazed by its height and girth as it rose to full mast again.

"Not really," Benny said. "But I can tell you that I only go a few days without such opportunities. We get a lot of tourists here."

"C'mon Benny! I said, a bit annoyed and quite frisky. I sat

up and straddled him. His cock was closer to reaching its full potential. I was rubbing it with both hands as I moved teasingly against him. "How many?"

"Child, please!" Benny said. "I feel too good to lie to you!"

"That's the whole point, Benny!" I said forcefully.

"Well," Benny said, "I've been doing this for three years. What I can say is that about halfway through, I lost track. Fifty, maybe."

"Fifty!" I said. "Wow Benny! Dan hasn't fucked more than, what, Dan, fifteen girls in his life? Right Dan?" Dan's smile was bitter, but his cock twitched even harder.

Benny laughed. "Well, I wouldn't know about that … but I can tell you that I counted my girls when I was a kid, and I hit 15 when I was 16 years old."

"Wow, Benny!" I said.

"Don't get carried away," Benny said. "It wasn't until I was 18 that I got with an older woman who taught me how to use what I had. Before then I was shy half the time, worried I would hurt the girls, not sure I knew how to make them happy."

"Lucky girls," I said to Benny, still stroking.

"Of course," Benny said, "Once I realized how to use what I had, then things got a bit more intense … and I stopped counting … and the girls kept coming … once one of their friends tried … word … got around."

"I'll bet it did," I said to Benny. I could feel my pussy dripping and the precum forming on his cockhead again. I rubbed it down the shaft. I was getting so wet thinking about Benny fucking his way through his youth, pleasing the girls who battled for his attention, while guys like my Dan with their small penises struggled to get laid.

"What was your hottest experience?" I asked Benny, stroking more intensely, gripping his shaft harder.

"Well … ohhhh, that's nice Linda … one really fun one: I was fucking an older woman who was divorced. Anyway, her youngest daughter came to the island for the summer, only

19, and she was just a goddess. Kind of looked like that blond
tennis girl who became a model ...."

"Anna Kournikova?"

"Yeah," Benny said, "kind of like her. Tall, blond, poison for
a guy like me."

I laughed.

"Anyhow," Benny said, "her mom didn't like the guy she was
dating. He was this spoiled rich guy who pulled attitude with
her and blew her off. She didn't want her daughter to end up
marrying him or even worse, getting knocked up somehow.
Her mom told me, 'You gotta fuck well when you're young,
worry about rich guys when you're older.' "

I laughed, slowly stroking Benny's cock up and down as I
listened to the story. "So what happened?"

"She asked me to seduce her daughter, to quote, 'Ruin
her daughter's pussy' for that guy. I said I would try, but her
daughter didn't seem like the kind you could easily seduce. You
couldn't just flash your cock at a girl like her. She needed more
warming up than that. Plus, when girls are that young, they
may be curious about big cocks but they aren't as aggressive.
They aren't really ...."

"Experienced?" I said.

"Yeah ..." Benny chuckled, seeming to recall the experience.
His dick seemed harder than before, with my hand running up
and down it. This girl must have really turned him on; even her
memory was bringing him to life.

"So what did you do?"

"Well, I tried to make friends with her over time," Benny
said. "Her mom had me around the house some, doing odd
jobs, mowing lawns. I didn't need the work, really, but I liked
the challenge. Her daughter wasn't all that flirty with me,
though.

"I told her mom it wasn't going to work out, that she was
pretty indifferent ... but her mom just told me to take my time.
She said that, a couple of times when I was walking around

in tight shorts, her daughter was definitely staring at my, uh, unit."

I chuckled at his use of "unit." I hadn't heard that word in a while.

"Once she thought she overheard her daughter saying something on the phone like 'His package is unreal,'" Benny said. "So she wanted me to keep at it.

"One night there was a turning point," Benny continued. "I was in the den in the back of the house, sleeping over because of a storm that knocked trees in the road. Her mom told me that this was the night. And before too long, her daughter did come in. Before I knew it, she was putting her hand on my cock. Next thing you know, we were making out on the couch.

"It still took me some kissing and sharing of secrets before she let me go farther ... but I did get inside of her and after that, it was on."

"Oh yeah?" I said, stroking away. "And did you ruin her pussy?"

Benny chuckled. "Well, not exactly ... but I knew as soon as I saw the surprised look in her eyes—when her pussy clenched and came on my cock—that she wouldn't ever be as happy with guys like her boyfriend again."

I laughed along with him. "No way!" I said, stroking Benny harder. My pussy was dripping again, thinking of that young blond goddess cheating happily on her boyfriend, pulling Benny deep inside her tan legs, not worrying about her boyfriend's small, ineffective penis or the consequences of getting fucked—in that moment, not even worrying about her mom hearing her ecstatic screams throughout the house.

"Enough talk!" I said while pushing Benny back on the towel. "I need it inside me again ...."

Benny's cock jutted out, not straight up but bending slightly, looking plump and scary. Dan's cock had to be rock hard to fuck well, but Benny .... As long as he was somewhat aroused there was plenty to work with. This time, I put the condom on, ripping the wrapper open with urgency, sliding it on fast, pushing Benny down hard, not thinking about Dan, grabbing for Benny's cock from behind. I lowered myself onto it, my hand on his brown chest as I guided it in. "Ah!" I said as I felt him slide into me. I started moving up and down on his cock, taking a good half of him inside me comfortably, loving that filled-up feeling.

I was up on that cock, getting used to it, feeling not only the pleasure of getting fucked, but a new, unaccustomed sensation: that if the penetration just kept up a little longer, a wailing pussy come was absolutely inevitable. Technique didn't matter. As long as Benny could stay reasonably hard—and boy, was he good at that—I was gonna come. I could just grind my way into the inevitable. No coaching or concentration needed, I could just let myself go. There was no losing Benny's cock.

This made me think of Dan, so I looked over at him, and was surprised to see him stroking his cock again, almost hard, watching me bounce up and down, obsessed with my greedy little pussy's needs.

I was disappointed in Dan; he was a good man, but he was sexually inferior to this stud fucking me so expertly. Cheryl was right, dammit—he was my emotional peer, but not my sexual peer. That's what Benny was. Whether I would lose Dan as a husband over this might be a pressing concern later, but until my pussy came again, that concern was completely irrelevant. Right now, it was all about this surge of pleasure between my legs, this amazing. baby-making fullness. I was moving up and down with urgency now, feeling my tits bounce and sway as Benny grabbed for them, brimming with lust and laughter.

"That's it, Dan, stroke your little dick," I said without mercy. "You could never fuck me like this, so you get to watch. Watch this pussy come again, watch how a real man fucks!"

"Oh yeah, baby! That's right! You tell him what you need!!" Benny encouraged me.

I would have more to say to Dan, but I couldn't think about

that now. I needed to come; I needed that more than anything. I could feel my pussy lips getting pulled inside out by his cock on every thrust. It was great to bounce like crazy without worrying about his cock slipping out—a constant concern with Dan.

I could feel the excitement rising inside, building and building. Benny could feel it too. "That's it, baby, you're really gonna come this time!"

Suddenly he grabbed my shoulders and held them tight, impaling me on his cock just as my pussy started spasming around him. My legs shook as I gave into a pleasure that ruled over right and wrong. "Oh my fucking God!!" I was trembling, leaning over his chest for balance, spasms gripping my body.

I thought I was all fucked out, but as I flopped down, Benny pulled me around and had my ass in the air. Before I could say otherwise, he was entering me from behind, kneeling to guide his huge head inside me.

But then he stopped and pulled out. "What Benny?"

"I was thinking ..." said Benny.

"What??!!" I said, moving my hips in nasty circles, humping my back out, searching impatiently for his cock.

"That maybe Dan would like to do the honors."

"Of what?" I asked.

"Of guiding me inside you."

I was shocked. I loved the idea.

"That's right, Dan, you do the honors. Take your hands of your little dick and come guide this man into me!"

Dan seemed in a trance, but he obeyed. His submission made my pussy drip like crazy. God I was a horny bitch!

I looked behind me as Dan grabbed Benny's thick cock and pushed his cockhead inside, where it landed with a loud, unDanlike plop.

"Oh wow, Benny, oh wow ...."

Benny starting moving his cock in and out of me from

behind. "Thank you, Dan," Benny said condescendingly. "I'll take it from here."

I laughed. Then I started to moan.

"That's it ..." he said encouragingly. "You have a gorgeous round ass ... stick it up in the air for me, show your husband how much you want this cock."

I did as I was told, moving my ass higher, seeking his cock.

Benny stuck it in deeper, responding to my movements. God it turned me on to be fucked by such a master cocksman. He gradually picked up the pace, and I felt myself coming again, sore but happy. "Coming!!" I said as he pounded me.

We slowed down for a bit, still fucking. I thought he would pull out and pronounce me well fucked. But he kept working it.

"That was nice Linda, but you have more for me."

"Oh I don't know, Benny, I'm pretty fucked out."

"No, I think you have a little more for me, a little more to show Dan."

"I don't know, Benny," I said as I turned around and smiled at him, so grateful for how he was making me feel.

"Let me show you, honey ...." And he grabbed the ends of my hair with one hand while steadying my hip with the other. He worked it a bit faster and it started to feel real good again, that warm itchy sensation dominating the soreness.

Then I heard a slamming sound and it was on!! I could feel the base of his cock against me, his entire dick inside of me.

"Oh! Oh!"

Benny was fucking me furiously now. It was so animalistic and violent the way he was pounding me. My pussy didn't even sound sexy, it sounded vulgar, like a plunger was ramming its way in with massive, slutty strokes.

"That's it, Linda!" Benny called out. "That's how you get fucked!"

"Oh my God, Benny! My pussy is on fire! This feels so good! Don't stop! Don't ever stop!"

Benny released my hair, gripped my hips, and really let me have it. Meantime my hair was flying around my mouth and face as I shook my head with passion and fucked my ass back as hard as I could.

"Fuck this cock, bitch! Show him what a slutty bitch you are!"

God, I couldn't believe he was talking to me like that! I loved every word of it. I couldn't have stopped fucking Benny if ten people had started watching.

"Tell him," Benny commanded. "Tell Dan what it's like!"

"Oh God, Dan!" I screamed. "This is how I need to get fucked! You have no idea how good this feels!"

Dan was working his little penis like crazy. He couldn't believe his eyes. He was lost in anger, shame, and lust. He was almost there.

"You could never fuck me like this, Dan! Your little dick would just slip out of my pussy! Isn't that true, Dan?" I yelled out, recalling some frustrating times when he had tried to take me doggy style and his cock had not been able to stay inside me once we started moving. The friction from Benny's cock was overwhelming by comparison.

"Look at it! Watch this big dick slide up in me, so deep, never falling out! That's what a woman needs!"

Dan was losing it. I was feeling that power Cheryl had told me about.

"That's it, Dan! Make that little dick come while your wife gets fucked! I wanna see you squirt! Squirt that little pee pee while you see what a real man can do to your wife's pussy!!" I couldn't believe how mean I was being to Dan, but it felt so natural, so right, and in a peculiar way, so kind.

Dan was helpless, totally in my control, although I wasn't even touching him. This turned me on even more. I watched his cock spurt and spurt, even though it didn't have much come left in it. Dan was on dry heaves at this point.

But then I forgot about Dan because Benny was fucking me

even harder, if that was possible, and it was all about Benny and what he was doing to my pussy, again and again, and then I felt something on its way out of my body, something so full and deep I didn't even recognize it until it splashed out of me:

"Oh God!! I'm cumming cumming cumming cumming ... CUMMING!!"

My pussy was turning inside out on Benny's cock, gripping and tugging and spasming. Benny just held me against his wonderful penis, my ass pulled high, until my spasms subsided. If he had rolled off his condom and put his sperm all up in my pussy I would not have protested. My juices were dripping all over my legs. I felt like the sluttiest whore ever ... and the happiest woman.

I wanted it to be over; I was sure it was over. Soreness was taking precedence over pleasure. Benny started pulling in and out again, nice and slow. It did feel kind of good, as though we were winding down—like lightly rubbing someone's back after a deeper massage.

"Oh, Linda, that was nice baby," Benny said.

"Benny, wow, yeah that was not so bad," I said teasingly, understating his prowess.

Benny seemed content to just move in and out slowly, his big hands resting calmly, possessively, on my hips, right in front of my husband.

And then it was over. I was finally fucked out. Benny's cock slipped out of me with a huge, drooling squelch.

This time, when the sex ended, there was no easy transition back to three friends on the beach. The scene had been a little too edgy. It was awkward as we cleaned up in silence and said our goodbyes, and even more uncomfortable after Dan and I went back to our hotel.

Chapter 14

Emotional Ramifications

❧

I WISH I COULD say that I apologized to Dan, or felt guilty, or worried about his feelings, but I really didn't. For the rest of the vacation, Dan was quiet and docile—very unlike him. All I could think about was fucking Benny as much as possible. I didn't invite Dan to watch again, but he always knew where I was going.

I found myself experiencing strange new emotions for Dan, even hostile ones. I started to think of him as pathetic. One day I came into the bathroom while he was in the shower and, seeing his penis so small and withdrawn, thought to myself, "Why did you marry a man with such a tiny cock?" Another time, I lay in bed, fingering my sore pussy, thinking it could use a little more fucking. Then I remembered I was with Dan, and I probably wouldn't even feel his skinny five-incher if he pushed it in as hard as he could, not with Benny stretching and filling me every day. Once Dan did try to fuck me, and I felt next to nothing. His small penis spurted quickly, as if it realized its hopeless task.

I did walk the beaches with Benny and Dan a couple more times. How people stared! Here we were, a living cliché. Me in the middle, with my small-dicked white husband on one side and this black man with a massive swinging penis on the other. A few people even tried to take pictures with us in the background. Perhaps even more intense were the times Benny and I walked the beaches alone. Girls would give me jealous glances. I could feel the guys stare at my fully-tanned body with intense lust, then glance at Benny's cock and look away, shy and embarrassed. It felt so right that I would be out with a huge fucker of a man who deserved my body sexually and was in no way intimidated by the prospect of pleasing my voracious pussy. But I was married, and vacations don't last forever.

After Dan and I got home from that trip, we lived almost like brother and sister—like brother and sister who weren't that fond of each other. I could feel us drifting. I wasn't sorry for what I had done; instead I felt sexually entitled. That anger and entitlement didn't mix well with Dan's sentiments. I had to wonder: "How will my marriage survive this?" Or ... "Should my marriage survive this?" I couldn't feel much of anything. All I could think about were these newfound needs my pussy had discovered, awakened by Eddie but brought to a turning point by Benny. I didn't think I could ever be satisfied by my husband again. For the first time, that previously unthinkable word, *divorce*, poked its way into my head.

I started fucking some guy on the side. The first time I got a big cock inside me again, it felt terrific. It was a relief to give into the sensations. But after the sex, things felt weird ... hollow ... bad.

Dan moved out a few days after. He packed a duffle bag, left a note with the hotel he was staying in. The note was short and factual, devoid of emotion. I got fucked again that night. After I came home, I ate a box of ice cream sandwiches, and cried my eyes out.

A couple weeks later, I found myself sitting on Cheryl's back porch. A part of me was secretly hoping Eddie was around, that I would get a little something. My heart sank when Cheryl said Eddie was out of town, or more accurately, my pussy pouted. What was I doing here anyway? But I couldn't talk to a therapist about this. Cheryl's unusual views on this topic seemed to make more bizarre sense than a therapist's anyway.

"Aww girl … buck up!" Cheryl said with that bubbly sisterhood vibe that immediately made me wish I hadn't come over.

"Dan moved out."

"Oh …. I'm sorry." She was silent, then: "Girl, you gotta get that boy back!"

"I know, but …."

One good thing about Cheryl: she wasn't going to give me the whole, "What about your daughter?" routine. I felt torn up enough already, even with her away at school.

"It's like this," Cheryl said. "Dan is a good husband and father. You don't want to let that go."

"Yeah …."

"Remember what I told you, that dirty little secret of female sexuality," said Cheryl.

"What's that?"

"Women need great sex *and* great love. There are very few men in this world who can provide both … and the best male lovers are rarely monogamous. Women fight over their prowess. Then we crank out a kid or two and settle for less sexually, or hope that being in love with someone will be enough, and sometimes it is, for a while … but it can grow stale. Then we cheat on our husbands and feel ashamed.

"I mean, look at me," Cheryl continued. "Eddie is an amazing fuck, as you know …." Cheryl stopped for a moment and smiled. "But I have no idea how I could raise a family with him. It really makes me nervous; that big dick of his could knock me up anytime." We both laughed, and I flushed, thinking of Eddie pounding into her.

"You have the opposite problem," Cheryl said. "You have great love, but your sex life has flatlined. Dan was all you needed at first, but now ..." Cheryl paused, perhaps to gauge my feelings, "his sexual shortcomings have become obvious to you."

I could only nod.

"He can make love to you, but he can't FUCK. And right now, your beautiful womanly body is in its sexual prime, and sometimes it needs to be FUCKED—by a man who is dominant enough to rip the come out of your body ... someone you can lose yourself to."

Her words alone were making me squirmy and hot. But then she took the lust back out of me: "You feel so little attraction to Dan that you are letting him drift away. But underneath that, you love him. Your life without him feels empty; your life with him feels compromised."

Cheryl had nailed it again ... what a pain she was. "Hey girlie, it could be worse," she continued. "A lot of women don't get good lovin' or good pushin'. At least we each have one of the two."

"But I want both!" I said. "And besides, I think you're better off. Without great sex, real romantic love is so ... difficult. You can always get your emotional needs met elsewhere."

"Yes ..." said Cheryl. "But there are plenty of loveless marriages. Sex fades too. Eventually, Eddie would become a distant partner. If we had kids, I'd be doing most of the work. Over time, his sexual appeal would fade as I became turned off by his indifference or angered by his cheating. He's not someone I would marry. Dan would die for you. I'd give anything to have a man like that in my life!"

I felt the rightness of what Cheryl was saying. Dan loved me enough to suffer intensely if that was the price.

"This is uncharted territory," said Cheryl. "You have to understand: women have never had the cultural and sexual power they enjoy today. They have always had to compromise. In some ancient societies I studied, women did exert more sexual power, but it wasn't common, and lack of birth control forced them into oppressive marriages sooner or later."

"We need new relationship forms," Cheryl went on. "Relationships that are structured on the understanding of women's pleasure and emotions."

"But how does that apply to me?" I asked Cheryl, feeling impatient and exasperated by her theoretical future.

"Well, think about the sexual psychology here," Cheryl said. "You need more than Dan can give you sexually. You know that, he knows that ...."

"Right ..." I said, wondering where this would lead.

"You're still equals in marriage, but you're not equal sexually."

"And remind me, why is that?"

"It's harsh but simple," Cheryl said: "Your pussy can make his cock come—easily, I might add—but his cock can't make your pussy come. And here's the kicker: you're in charge of any man sexually who can't make your pussy come. Your best orgasms usually come when you're submitting to a man who can fill you up, the kind of man who makes you want to spread your legs so he can stretch you and make you shake and turn you inside out."

"But Dan *can* make me come," I protested weakly.

"Yes, but you have to be in the mood," Cheryl said. "You have to work at it. He has to stimulate your clit while you tell him what adjustments to make ... whereas, a guy like Eddie, if he puts his big cock inside you, you are coming no matter what."

I was annoyed with her again. What a shallow way to think—but she was dead on right.

"You are sexually dominant over anyone who doesn't have the ability to make you come," said Cheryl. "Dan can't make you submit to your inner slut like these studs can, and his inability to prey on your submissiveness puts him in an inferior category. Especially since you can make him come at will, just by gripping your pussy around his inadequate penis. So you and Dan are no longer sexual equals, and you have to accept that.

"But here's the thing," she continued. "Dan knows this, too… he senses his sexual place. He craves it. He wants you to put him there. Deep inside, there's nothing he wants more than to hear that he is sexually inferior to you, and that you need a real Alpha male to satisfy you—which he is not."

I had nothing to say; it was a lot to absorb. Cheryl had alluded to these subjects before, but this time her words were really sinking in.

"We each have our sexual destinies," Cheryl continued. "You are an alpha girl. As such, you crave submission to the rare male who can really take you over. This is a primal need inside you, driven by your desire to be impregnated. Your pussy is in charge of this process, not your head, and your pussy knows that pregnancy can best happen with a large cock opening up your vagina, spreading it wide with orgasms, and then shooting a big load deep inside you, all up against your walls." I felt squirmy and horny just listening to her talk like this!

"Now that you've had this experience," said Cheryl, "no vow of monogamy will protect you—unless you're getting what you need inside the relationship. That 'pussy memory' of being stretched, filled, orgasmed, inseminated—for that you'll throw everything to the wind, you'll cheat on Dan, you'll do whatever it takes to get that feeling again, those baby-making orgasms, screaming on a nice thick cock. But here's the thing: after that need passes, you will crave love and affection again, and to be taken care of. In a way, you need two different men, or one man who is incredibly versatile in his physical and emotional skills."

How did Cheryl know so much more about what made me tick than I did?

"But it gets more interesting," Cheryl said. "You also have a need to put submissive men in their places, and that's why you're so attached to one."

"But Dan's not submissive!" I said.

"No, in the outside world he's not. He's not a total submissive;

he's what they call a 'switch.' But deep down, he knows he's a beta man in the bedroom—a beta boy." Cheryl's words were harsh, but she didn't sound cruel, just truthful. "He needs you to show him his sexual place; you both crave that on some level. And you love claiming that power over a man who seems, to the outside world, like he would never surrender that power. Yet you can take it, use it, put him in his place with it. And he needs that more than anything—until the point where it takes away from his self-respect. That's why your cheating has driven him off.

"It won't be easy," Cheryl continued, "but the best hope for your relationship is to live out these needs, either in fantasies or real life …. I'll bet if you talk about this honestly again, your sexual spark will come back. It might be different than it once was, when you were so in lust with Dan you saw him as your sexual equal, but it will give a spark back to your sex life, and Linda, it just might be the best hope for your marriage. You may even find him surprising you with a different kind of confidence—one based on acceptance and not on the pressure of having to perform beyond what he is genetically capable of."

"If it's just about size, why don't we get some big toys?"

"Well, playing with toys can be good and a great outlet for fantasies," said Cheryl. "But I think you will find toys don't get to the heart of it. It's not just about size; it's about size as an avenue into dominance and submission. If Dan puts a large toy in you, he's still a small-dicked guy pushing a toy into you. He's not taking over your body, and your pussy isn't juicing up the way it would with a big guy totally taking it over."

I could definitely remember that super wet feeling, which allowed me to take these dicks that seemed so much larger than what I could normally handle.

"That's why you generally can take a bigger cock than a toy," Cheryl continued. "Using a toy doesn't allow you to experience total submission nor does it allow Dan to experience the wonderfully intense feelings of being put in his place by you sexually. And I think you'll notice, the best sex is sex that you share, where everyone is finding their place at the same time, where the truth of what you need is sharp enough to hurt a little. The physical sensations of being filled with a big cock are almost a bonus compared to the sacrifice, the proof of love Dan is offering you, and the rush of submitting totally to one man and dominating another at the same time."

"Wow." It was all I could think of to say. But she was right—those orgasms had been the most intense of my life. I suddenly realized it wasn't just Benny's size that made them so incredible—it was the way I had simultaneously taken charge of Dan's sexual pleasure. Even while having sex with Benny alone, Dan had been on my mind. Knowing how much these encounters were making him crazy drove me to new heights.

"Don't screw this up by longing for the perfect man," said Cheryl. "The perfect man is just that, and almost impossible to find, even for sexy smart girls." Cheryl's inviting look made me want to throw her on the ground myself. "Bring the father of your child home, and set this right. It won't be a simple relationship, but it's your best chance."

Silence on my end.

"You know you deserve this ..." Cheryl added. "Why else would you have felt so little guilt fucking Benny all week?"

I forgot I had told Cheryl about that, and blushed.

"God, that big black cock must have felt so good inside you," Cheryl said a little wistfully.

"Oh ... you have no idea ..." and we started laughing. The hard part of the conversation was over; the rest was girl talk, lusty girl talk. I had a lot to think about. I stayed up late, sitting on the front porch and listening to the wind bend the trees.

CHAPTER 15

SEX VERSUS LOVE VERSUS SEX

❧

THE NEXT FEW DAYS without Dan were strange, hollow. His absence was an indictment of my choices. I kept hoping to get horny, for lust to overpower the loneliness, but it didn't happen. I masturbated a couple of times, but the orgasms were halfhearted. I thought about visiting Dan at his hotel, begging him to come homedrop , kissing him into submission, feeling his arms wrapping around my back and knowing that his eyes regarded me with real love. But something stopped me.

Two weeks went by; then one day I got home from work and saw Dan's CRV parked outside. I heard a rustling in the garage and knew he was in there rummaging around. Before he could say anything, I was kissing him, holding him, pulling him into the living room. We lost ourselves in the moment, putting aside recent history. The next day, I woke up in his arms, feeling a rightness creeping back into my world. Why was I ever stupid enough to question it?

"Dan?"

"Yeah."

"Dan, I don't know all the answers, and I'm starting to think

I never will. But I do know I'll be making a really big mistake if I let you go. I want you to come home."

"Okay."

Dan's first week back was almost like a honeymoon. We were in a rhythm—even making breakfast was dreamy, with Dan cooking my eggs with just the right amount of runny yolk—a skill that had eluded him in the past. He even warmed my slippers by the heater so that they would be ready for me when I got out of the shower.

The second week was less dreamy; we were back in our old marital comfort zone. The third week, I had my first confusing thought. Parts of my conversation with Cheryl were sneaking back.

"Linda …."

Dan was waking me up. It was early in the morning.

"Yeah, honey? Is something wrong?"

"Yes."

"What?" I said, sitting up now, instantly wide awake.

"We have a problem."

"We do?"

"Yeah … I'm not sure …" Dan continued, "that we can go on without a sex life of some kind."

"But we had sex, just the other day," I protested.

"Actually that was a week ago."

"Oh," I said.

"I had time to think about this while I was gone," Dan said. "This isn't going to be easy for me to say…."

I sat straight up in bed, fearing the worst.

"I don't think we are sexually compatible," he said.

"Oh, nonsense!" I said. "We have great sex sometimes …."

"No," he said. "I think our marriage is going to die a slow death without the brutal truth …. So here it is …."

I waited.

"I think you need a much bigger cock than I have. I'm too small to satisfy you."

I felt a flash of anger and embarrassment. Everything in my head—every progressive intellectual thought, every drop of common sense, every feeling of hope for the future—told me Dan was wrong. But the twitch between my legs told me something else.

"Dan, there are plenty of ways to satisfy a woman, you know that .... And you're good at a heck of a lot of them."

"Linda, you forget, I was there. I watched you—not once, but two different times with two different guys .... I saw how you responded to them physically."

I was embarrassed into silence. I couldn't see where this was headed, or how it could help us.

"But there's something more, Linda, something I haven't told you."

"What's that?"

"You weren't the only one who needed that; I needed it, too. I needed you to be honest about my inability to fuck you properly. I needed you to tease me about my little dick ... and ... here goes: tell me how lucky a small-dicked guy like me is to have such a beautiful woman as you as his wife—a woman who can get just about any man she wants."

I sat there and stewed on his words, quietly flabbergasted. It was a bold confession, very much in line with what Cheryl had said. I felt torn between the sexually correct ideas in my head and that persistent tug between my legs.

"So how does this help us?" I asked Dan. "Let's say that what you say is true ... how does it help us? Doesn't it just show that we need to break up, or as you were saying, that we are incompatible?"

"Well ..." said Dan. "That's what I thought ... but now I'm not so sure anymore .... See, I got to thinking ... the guys you fucked—the ones who pleased you so well—I really don't think you would ever want to date those guys seriously, much less marry them."

"Oh God, no!" I said.

"And well, let's face it: it would be very hard for me to find a relationship as good as this one, with a woman as amazing as you are."

"Well, I don't know about that," I responded, a little self-consciously.

"So ..." Dan persisted, "I think we need to ... I don't know ... come to an arrangement."

"An arrangement?"

"Yeah. An understanding that I have trouble pleasing you, that it's the only flaw in our marriage. The thing is; it can become a huge fault line if we don't face it. So we acknowledge it openly, have fun with it, stay honest ...."

I was thinking.

"Maybe that means you have sex with other guys sometimes while I watch, maybe that means trying bigger toys to see if that does the trick. But we start with honesty, brutal sexual honesty, and let that dictate our choices. This way, maybe we find that spark, and no one cheats. Maybe no one gets hurt."

I didn't know what to say. I didn't even know how to think about it. But maybe there was something to it: Cheryl's advice and Dan's ideas had a lot of common ground.

"Dan, can I think about this for a while?"

"Sure, no problem .... I'm going to get ready for work."

Chapter 16

An Opportune Disruption

❦

IT WAS FASCINATING TO be around Dan the next couple of weeks. He had a weight off his shoulders and some swagger in his step. I wasn't particularly attracted to him, but he didn't seem pathetic, either. "Brave" was the word that came to mind. Brazen in his love for me. Meanwhile, I drooped around the house. I'd come home from work, hit the TV couch, and devour whatever snacks I could find. But Dan, he was a man at peace with himself, and what's more, he seemed comfortable with my own indecision. We didn't have sex, but there was no pressure from him, no hint of dissatisfaction. I didn't know what to do exactly, but I felt comfortable around him.

I'm not sure how long this new arrangement would have lasted, but events intervened to put a stop to it after three and a half weeks.

The event that marked three and a half weeks occurred in an unexpected way. I was asked by my boss to entertain a potential client. Most of these guys were schlubs, burnouts worn down from years on the road. Steve, however, was not. As soon as I saw him, I felt a jolt. It was odd, because he was rather short, perhaps 5 foot 7, shorter than me. But he had a way about him, and a heavy masculine voice.

He stared straight into my eyes, his gaze unwavering. It was the kind of look that said, "I could have you if I wanted you." I wasn't used to that; I was used to being able to intimidate guys from the outset—especially my drab work colleagues.

It was easy to be careless with Steve, to share a drink over dinner, something I never did with clients. To share another drink. To sit in my car with him after dinner, to kiss him. Then to pull away.

"Steve, I can't do this. I'm ... married."

"Linda, I'm not looking to break up your marriage," said Steve in that mesmerizing deckhand voice. "I'm just looking to make you feel good. I want to make you feel ... like the hot lady you are."

Steve's lines were kind of bland, really. Dan was much more poetic. But Steve's powerful voice overcame his weak material.

"Steve, I just .... My husband and I have had some ups and downs recently. I just can't do this right now to our marriage .... We're finally coming out the other side ...."

"Okay, Linda, I understand," Steve said with a crack of a smile. "But the thing is, I can tell how bad you want it, so something isn't right ...."

What an asshole. I drove Steve back to his car, steamed over this last remark. Who did he think he was? What arrogance! I thanked him for dinner in a dismissive way and drove off with my foot on the gas.

But in bed later that night, after Dan was asleep, I masturbated for the first time in a long while, and had a warm, tingly come ... thinking about Steve.

I didn't want to admit it, but I was disappointed when I learned that Steve had left town, that another person would be taking over. Two weeks later, when I learned that Steve was coming back into town to sign the paperwork, I tingled with anticipation.

Before I knew it, we were making out like teenagers again, this time in Steve's rental car. He guided me into the back seat, his hand on my breast, mine on his crotch. I had known from the start Steve had a big cock—his effortless confidence pretty much guaranteed it—and there it was, all bunched up in a huge wad. I had to push his hands off me to take a closer look, unzipping him, pulling out his half-hard dick, gasping a bit. Steve wasn't the biggest guy I had seen, but he had this thick root jutting into a huge mushroom head. On his small frame, it looked enormous. His cock felt crazy thick in my hands, and it wasn't even hard yet.

"Oh wow, Steve ... Oh wow," I said as I started jerking him off, looking to see if anyone was around. But the parking lot behind the restaurant was deserted.

"Yes Linda, Yes. Feel it, that's for you, all of that is for you."

I couldn't help but stroke it, see if I could make it rise. What a difference this was from my tender affections with Dan. With Steve, I felt so ... intimidated, like I'd been thrown in the ring with a sexual force that pushed me to my limits.

"Oh Steve ...." Steve's cock pushed out aggressively from his body, its mushroom head swollen and red. It wasn't what you would call a beautiful cock, far from it. Dan's small slender cock was much more elegant. But Steve's cock ... it's a cock that could do some damage, I thought as I jacked it up and down. It had a strange shape—incredibly thick at the shaft, tapering off right at the head before expanding into that big mushroom. It wasn't the longest cock I'd seen—though quite a bit longer than Dan's—but the thickness and strange shape set it apart. I was on the verge of throwing everything I had with Dan away, imagining ways to get that cock inside me, but something stopped me. Surprising even myself, I knew what I had to do.

"Steve, you remember I'm married, right?"

"Yes, and remember that I said ...."

"Steve, the point is this: I'm not going to cheat on my

husband. Not now, not ever. But ... his cock is really small, and sometimes I need a cock like yours ...."

Steve looked confused. I kept stroking him to get the conversation where I wanted it.

"I want to talk to Dan ... let him know I met someone with a nice manly cock .... And Steve, if Dan wants to watch it happen, I want him to."

Steve didn't seem to fancy these complications, but I looked good that night. Tight fitting skirt, a pink tube blouse that clung to me more than it should have, some tanned cleavage jutting out .... Steve wanted me as much as I wanted him ... and he would do anything I said.

"Well, Linda, if that's what it's gonna take to get inside of you, that's what it's going to take."

"So you'll do it?"

"Yeah," said Steve, "I'll do it. But what if Dan says no?"

"Oh, he'll say yes," I smiled wickedly. "Besides, he doesn't have much of a choice." I could feel the truth of that revelation jolting up and down my body. "Just come by my house tomorrow night at eight o'clock."

"Okay. But can you at least do something about my blue balls?" Steve asked.

I felt like I had to help him out there. Cupping his huge balls with my left hand, or trying to, I jacked him off with my right, stroking and rubbing. I could barely wrap my hand around his shaft, but I loved gripping him, thinking about all that thickness pressing into me. I jacked him up and down in a frenzy, eager to make him come before I did something I would regret.

At the end, I was dripping so much thinking about him stretching me that if he had thrown me down in the back seat, I would have spread my legs and opened my pussy up for him, without even demanding a condom. But he didn't know that, so I stroked him like mad. Soon he came in big messy bursts, all over his clothes and on me. It never ceased to amaze me how much sperm seemed to come out of these big cocks. It felt unfair that Dan wasn't able to spray like that, but then again, it felt so right that a big studly cock would come in such big spurts for me.

Dan ... speaking of Dan, I would have to do something about him.

CHAPTER 17

GETTING WHAT I WANT MEANS GETTING WHAT

HE WANTS

WHEN I ARRIVED HOME, Dan was already crashed out. I wanted to wake him, but I was soothed by his trust. He felt no need to stay up, to question my whereabouts. The next morning I was awake before him, taking a shower. After the shower, I looked at myself in the mirror. I wished I had more of a washboard stomach; it was hard getting used to my full hips and rounded tummy. But for whatever reason, today in particular, I could see why a lot of men seemed to like my body better now than when I was an athletic beanpole. My breasts weren't as firm as the teenage version of me, but they were full and heavy, and my hips …. well, they were something for a man to dig into, to lose himself in …..

I walked back to bed and woke up Dan.

"Dan, I have to talk with you."

"Oh yeah? What about?"

Suddenly, I surprised myself. My sluggishness from previous weeks had lifted. The way I had held back last night, refusing to take the step that might wreck my marriage, had given me a fresh attitude. I was a different person this morning, *a different woman.* "Dan, I invited Steve over tomorrow night."

"Okay, sure …."

"But Dan, not for dinner. To fuck me. Steve has a big thick cock and I want to feel it inside me. I need to feel my pussy filled and stretched again, and I need you to be there. It won't be right if you aren't there to watch it happen."

There was a huge, massive, marriage-ending silence in the room. Each second felt like a minute. Five seconds, ten.

But the marriage didn't end …. "Okay Linda, Okay." He paused. "But Linda?"

"Yes Dan?"

"Did you fuck him already?"

"Well, honey, I almost did, but it wasn't right. I wanted you to know how much I respect you and that I will *not* risk losing you for the sake of lust. Like you said: I want to see how much honesty our marriage can hold. I want to know if that can save us."

Dan grabbed me, held my face close to his, looked me boldly in the eye, and said, "Thanks." We cuddled for a while; I think I even cried a bit. I felt closer to him than I had in a long time, told him so. For a moment, I felt a reprieve from these desires that had upended my life and our marriage.

"Me, too …." Dan said. "Me too …."

Before I knew it, a warm loving feeling was sweeping over me and Dan was between my legs eating me out so nicely, licking me, consuming me. I had a sweet orgasm, rising up to his face, pulling him closer. My hips trembled up to meet him.

The next morning, Dan left for work, a bit late but with a reawakened look, leaving me in bed. I couldn't imagine wanting to have an orgasm ever again. But half an hour later, I put down my book and realized I needed to come again. I dug into myself with my fingers, only this time, it was Steve driving me on. I left for the office feeling relaxed, but worked up at the same time. I wondered how I would feel after tonight.

I won't lie; it felt strange having dinner at our place, the three of us: Dan, me, and the guy who was going to fuck me. I almost lost my nerve in the middle of that awkwardness. Dan and Steve were feigning politeness, but they were also at odds, competing in some subliminal undertow.

I was the one who grabbed Steve's hand and led him to the bedroom, buzzed from the wine. But my boldness didn't come from the alcohol. It came from my swaying hips, the delicious power they held over Dan and Steve. *I'm going to get my brains fucked out, and Dan is going to love it just as much as I am.* Or almost as much, and he wasn't going to give me any grief about the difference.

With no further thought of Dan, I was on my knees, latching onto Steve's cock, which was nearly hard as I wrenched it from his pants. In a way that felt more loving than cruel, I instructed Dan to sit down and take out his little penis. "Dan, I want you to savor every stroke of this, the pleasure I get out of it. Got it honey?"

"Oh yes …" Dan said, "Oh yes." He was sitting in the lounge chair we had brought in for this occasion. The situation might sound odd as I type it, but in the moment, it felt completely natural.

Steve smiled at Dan. I could see him stifling a laugh, but he decided not to act the jerk; I was glad he didn't. Soon he was moaning as I took that big head into my mouth, taken by the fullness and his forceful pushing on the back of my head, so hard I almost choked.

"Yeah suck that cock bitch, suck it good." Steve was going a nasty route, but with my husband looking out for me, it felt safe to have these slutty feelings with a virtual stranger.

"Oh Steve … it's … it's a monster …" I said, jerking his shaft with one hand, rubbing myself a little and swaying.

"Fuck it!" He pushed me forcefully back on the bed. "I'm fucking that pussy that's been teasing me for weeks now."

"But Steve, I'm not warmed up. I'm not ready," I protested.

"Oh you'll be ready," Steve said. "You'll be ready."

He yanked my plaid skirt down quickly, forcing it off my

thighs, buttons popping. The panties came next, quickly, forcefully.

He reached into his pocket and pulled out a condom, kicking his pants to the floor.

"Put this condom on my cock, bitch, so I can make you my slut!" Steve said. I don't know what was hotter—Steve talking to me that way in front of my husband, or the fact that he was taking the time in the middle of being such a prick to thoughtfully get out a condom.

I sat up, took the condom off, and rolled it over his fat cock, which was so swollen the condom was tight. His fat head was practically busting the seams. The condom didn't make it down to the base. God, but these cocks that were too big for condoms made my pussy drool!

He pushed me down and spread my legs, one in each hand, parting them wide.

"But Steve—you're not going to eat me out first? I don't know if I'm ready for you! I'm not used to such a fat cock!" I protested.

"Oh you're ready …" Steve said confidently, sticking his finger inside me. "You're so wet for my cock. You want to feel it stretching you out. You can get your pussy eaten some other time when you don't have a big cock around."

I wanted to look over at Dan and see how he felt about that, but before I could, Steve pushed that bloated mushroom head inside me, and I looked up with a jolt.

"Oh wow, Steve, wow!"

"Yeah, you're ready," Steve said. "Just a bit of in and out and you'll be begging for the whole thing."

"Mmm …."

Steve was thrusting in and out, deliberately but not too deep. I could feel my pussy lips scraping and gripping on that mushroom head, not sure whether to wrap around it or push it back out. That big head made plopping sounds as my pussy lips reluctantly let it go and then took it in again. I began thrusting, and Steve started moving, keeping his cockhead inside me. I came a little, just from the amazing sensations.

The thrusting intensified, and I definitely came then, my pussy spasming in little bursts. "Oh God, Steve, that was nice," I said.

"You want me to keep going?" he asked.

"Yes ...."

That's when he pounded me deeper, fuller ... pushing my legs even wider, mashing between me.

I instinctively grabbed the strong muscles in his butt and pulled him into me.

"Yes, Steve! Yes! Fuck me with that big dick of yours!!"

"Oh you love it, don't you, slut?"

"Damn, Steve, I do!! I do!!"

I couldn't say much more; my pussy was in control, yelling and screaming in a language of its own, clinging gratefully to that wonderful thick cock as it steamed in and out of me. His cockhead was pushing all over my insides, in a violent quest for my orgasm, with just enough skill to pull it out of me.

Before I knew it, I was spasming on the bed, his cock half inside me and the thrusts winding down. I sighed, and then moaned, "no!" when Steve pulled his cock out of me, making a big wet plopping sound.

"Roll over, slut; I'm not done with you yet!"

Obediently, practically in a trance, I did as he said.

"Now," he commanded. "Back it up, but move this way, so your husband has a better view."

Oh yeah, my husband! I had forgotten about him. Steve moved me sideways on the bed. If I looked to the left, I could see Dan sitting on the other side, stroking his crazy hard erection.

Steve penetrated me from behind, standing back from the bed to give Dan a clear view of Steve's cock pushing inward.

"Jeez, Steve, careful with that thing," I pleaded. I would never get used to that big head when it first poked in.

"Oh it's fine! You're ready for it, all wet for it."

Slowly, expertly, he started thrusting in and out.

I moved my hips in a circular motion, taking more of him in.

"Ahh ..."

"You see, Dan?" Steve said, looking over at my husband. "Women are full of it. They tell me I'm an asshole when I hit on them, but sooner or later, they want this dick, they want to get fucked ... doesn't matter if they're married or single."

"Oh it's true, Dan," I said, looking over at him. "There's nothing like this feeling ... nothing."

Dan was stroking, loving this talk. I took it further.

"That's it, Dan, stroke that little dick! You like it, don't you? You like to see him please me!"

"Oh yeah ..." Dan said, totally into our game.

"This is why we're here, Dan, because your little cock can't fill me up ... You want to hear how good his cock feels?"

"Yes!" said Dan. Unlike in the past, I didn't see shame in his eyes, only desire.

"God, it feels so much better than yours. You know how you slip out, and when you don't ..." (I gasped in mid-thrust) "I can't usually feel it ..." (another thrust!) "But I can feel this, Dan!"

Dan was stroking harder now.

"Dan, he's gonna make me cum if he fucks me harder, do you want to see him make me cum? Cum like you can't?"

"Oh God, yes!!" called out Dan, almost in a state of ecstasy.

"C'mon Steve!" I called out. "Fuck me. Show my husband how a real man makes me cum!"

Steve picked up the pace, grabbing my ass with both hands and pulling me to him savagely. Sweat formed on my back as we picked up the action, two animals who knew nothing of each other except how to do this one thing, this one perfect primal thing. I bucked my ass up to him desperately, clinging and pounding at the base of his cock as he gave it to me.

Meanwhile my husband watched in a state of jealous arousal, sparking me to raise my ass higher, knowing it tortured Dan to see my round ass bucking like that, when I had so often expelled his small penis in the same process. But not Steve!

Steve's dick was so intense. I could feel my pussy lips tugging at him as he pounded me, deeper and deeper. I could feel his cockhead pushing me to my limits, just on the verge of unacceptable pain, but not quite! And then I felt that hot itch, bucking up through my ass, feeling it getting scratched, hot and restless and nasty. This time the cumming was deep inside me, and Steve was just ripping into me to get it, pounding his balls on quick, deep thrusts, yanking my hair back from the roots, hurting as he pulled but I didn't care, I just needed this cum!

It seemed like the fucking went on and on, each stroke harder than the last, until I felt this massive warmth surging through me. This is what it was like to get fucked so well, so *fucking* well. This is why a girl like me submits so totally, in desperate search of this one feeling she can't find herself, this total submission ... to this moment and ....

"I'm cumming Steve!! Oh God!!!" I was shaking and bucking and screaming and losing myself. Steve's fat cock held my pussy tight as I spasmed around it, not letting me lose him or lose the sensations until my enormous vaginal cum had subsided.

As my hips finally slowed their rotation, Steve pulled his cock out with another signature nasty plop. Without losing a beat, still horny as all get out, I pulled the condom off his cock and started jerking him hard, kneeling in front of him and rubbing his balls.

"That's it, Steve, give it to me, give it to me!" Steve was right there on the edge.

"Steve, empty those balls for me, let's see it!" Steve started moaning and pulling me closer as ropey strings of cum started lapping at my breasts, pushing out of his manly cock with such force it seemed a shame to waste it. He shot off while Dan and

I watched, in awe of this big spurting cock that had such power over my grateful pussy.

"God, Steve, I am soaked in cum!" I told him.

I went into the bathroom to towel it off. Steve went in next and turned on the shower.

CHAPTER 18

INADEQUACY AS A TURN ON

∽

D AN PLOPPED IN BED beside me, his cock also spent from coming. I realized with some chagrin that I wasn't done coming yet; I was still more Steve's whore than Dan's wife. I started masturbating myself, legs spread, brazen and slutty on the bed.

"Did you like it, Dan?" I asked him as I rubbed myself, tweaking my clit between my fingers. "Did you like to see me screaming like that?"

"Oh, yeah!" Dan said.

"Let's see!"

I switched to rubbing with my left hand so I could stroke Dan with my right. His cock felt so small and soft in my hands. It twitched instantly when I touched it.

"Oh …" was all Dan could say.

"Yes, Dan, your little cock likes this, likes to see my pussy get filled! Doesn't it Dan?" I didn't need an answer as his cock sprang to life.

"Oh, yes, it does!" I said to Dan, still mystified by how this truthful talk felt more loving than cruel.

My cunt twitched.

"Dan, I'm going to need some more fucking soon … do you think your tiny cock can do anything for me?"

"Oh hell, yes!" Dan said. I loved his newfound confidence.

Then I had a wicked thought. A couple of Steve's Trustex XL condoms were lying around (I loved it when Steve told me that even Magnum XLs were too tight for his thickness). I unwrapped one and rolled it over Dan's cock. I laughed; I couldn't help myself. Dan's little cock swimming in plastic was quite a sight. There was a bunch of extra latex at the top of the condom, and width-wise, it was loose as heck, even though Dan's cock was as rock hard as I'd ever seen it.

"Go for it Dan! Let's see what you can do!"

Dan seemed determined to prove me wrong. Mounting me, holding the base of the condom, he started pushing it into me.

"Are you in, Dan?" I honestly wasn't sure. I also knew it would get him riled up.

He was pissed. "Yeah it's in, and I'm gonna fuck you with it!" Dan started pushing in and out, but holding the condom by its base was messing up his rhythm.

"No cheating, Dan!" I said to him as I pushed his hand away.

"Fine!" He called out, pissed and ready to make me pay for it with a solid pounding. I spread my legs for him as he pushed, then grabbed me underneath and started pounding me hard.

"Oh, Dan!" I called out. "I can feel you hitting me!" The base of Dan's cock was mashing me as he pounded like a madman. I could feel him channeling all the frustrations of his inadequacies into this frenzied, pounding fuck.

"Ha, ha!" I called out to Dan, "The condom slipped right off!" And it was true. The condom had fallen off and was lying near my belly. Dan reached down and swatted it away, kept on pounding me. He was rabid; I loved his fierceness. I couldn't feel him all that well until he hit my pubic bone with his deepest thrusts, but I could feel that! It was hot to see him pounding me, giving me back all the trash talk I had given him.

I wasn't going to cum like this, not without rubbing my clit, but he was fucking way too fast for that, and it felt great. I admired his unapologetic attitude.

But I wasn't done with him yet. "Fuck me, Dan. Is that all you've got? Fuck me!" I challenged him, frustrated that he wasn't big enough to rock my world like Steve.

"Pound me with that little dick! If you can make me come, I'll send Steve home! Pound me!" He was not going to hold up under this kind of teasing, but he pounded me crazily. "Dan, that little dick is gonna squirt! Squirt inside of me, Dan! Let my pussy suck that little pee pee dry!"

Maybe it was that final "pee pee" comment, but Dan couldn't help himself—he squirted and shook. A guy that could usually fuck forty-five minutes straight couldn't handle ten minutes when I mocked him like that. But I loved the control.

"Oh Dan, that was great!" I said to him, smiling. Dan looked down at me, torn between pride and shame. I wasn't ready to comfort him, so I kept up the cruel kindness. He needed to be put in his place, and I was going to do it.

But before I could finish that thought, Steve was applauding behind us. He had finished his shower.

"That was a great show," Steve said. Then he surprised us: "You have a sincere marriage. I haven't seen many like it. I hope to find the kind of connection the two of you have someday. It takes a lot of trust to be able to talk the way the two of you were talking to each other just now. And it took a lot of trust to bring me here."

"Thanks Steve," I stammered, not really knowing what to say, surprised by his admission.

Steve reached for his pants, sensing it was time to leave us alone.

"Steve, don't go yet," Dan said.

I looked over at Dan in wonder.

"She needs a little more," Dan said. A silence, then, "A little more ... from you.

"I got her worked up, to a point," Dan went on. "But we all know what she needs now."

Steve's smile was proud, but more open than it had been earlier. "But I already showered," he protested.

"Ah, c'mon Steve, don't you want inside this pussy again?" I said, pushing my legs wide and rubbing my hands down them invitingly, enticing him with my lips. I could see the tan lines of my stomach leading down to my legs, toned, sweaty, ready for more. What guy could resist?

"Aw fuck!" Steve said, reaching for a condom.

I got another nasty idea.

"Wait, Steve!" I said. And I reached into the drawer for one of Dan's condoms that we rarely used.

"I want to see how you fit in here," I said, unzipping the condom.

"Oh fuck, no!" said Steve. "Those are way too tight for me!"

"Please, Steve? Dan and I would love to see the contrast in sizes ...."

Without giving him a chance to change his mind, I was up and on my knees in front of him, slobbering on his head, licking it, stroking him at the base, marveling at its thickness. I felt so submissive in front of Steve. My pussy started wetting up again.

"Ahhh ..." was all Steve could say as I coaxed his erection back to life, setting the condom down so I could work his heavy balls with one hand and stroke him with the other. Then, with a "fuck me" look straight in the eyes and some rubbing of his engorged head on my tits, he was mine.

I unwrapped the condom, tried to get it over his swollen head.

"Wow, Steve, that's a tight fit," I said, my pussy squirming at the sight. I rolled the condom on farther, and finally over the head. When it was on, he and I both laughed. It only covered half the shaft, threatening to burst at any moment.

"Look Dan," I said, peering over the bed at him. "A cock like Steve's—a real man's cock—is waaay too big for your condoms."

Dan didn't say anything, but I could see his cock twitch from across the room as he stroked it in his hand, straining toward hard again.

Steve was a little rough as he pushed me down. Even an hour ago, I wouldn't have liked it, but we had a rhythm now. Steve made me want to be even more of a slut, to show Dan how dirty I could be.

Steve forced my legs apart. I resisted, but only to feel his power. He forced my legs wide and jammed himself in, which was possible only because I was so wet. "Oh!!"

The one thought I had time for was how incredibly different the two cocks I'd had inside me today had felt .... Then I was off, and Steve was off, pounding me to oblivion. I was thrusting into him, pulling his ass closer, and he was giving it to me so hard I couldn't think about Dan or how to include him right now. This was all about a big inevitable cum screaming out of my pussy and there it was ....

"Oh fuck, Steve, my pussy's gonna cum, all over your cock!!"

"That's it Linda, cum for me, cum for me," Steve said, calmly, like a tour guide. He clamped me up against the base of his cock, lifting my ass off the bed before the spasms from my pussy tried to throw me off his cock. But he held me in there deep, and my spasms pulsed through. Before I was even done, he was fucking me again.

"Steve, that hurts. I'm not sure if I can take any more of this today."

"Yes you can, you fucking slut! Yes you can!"

I tried to pull back from Steve, but he was too strong. "Oww! That hurts!" I said, worried that my pleasure had really turned into pain.

But almost as soon as I said it, I could feel the pain subside. I felt so full, so intensely feminine. Looking over at my husband stroking his little dick so feverishly, I wondered what my sister would think, my neighbors! Before I knew it, I was pushing my pussy back up to Steve once again, searching for one more orgasm.

Steve started to slow down. "I'm not sure the condom is going to last much longer," he said.

"Oh fuck, I don't care Steve, I don't fucking care!"

And with that, he resumed his heavy thrusting, slamming into me .... But then it happened: a *snap!* The condom was coming off his cock in bits and pieces.

"Just take it off and keep going, Steve, don't fucking stop now! I don't care if you knock me up, just keep going!" (I found out later Dan came right then, stroking his cock in a frenzy that left him with some cockburn afterwards, but I barely noticed him). Steve was giving me everything he had, his abs dripping with sweat. Then he pushed me all the way down, and I just moaned and moaned. I wasn't sure what was happening and then I felt it—the wonderful, until now unimaginable sensation of sperm splashing all over the backs of my pussy walls. It was such a rush. I started erupting. I had never felt Dan's spurts on the walls of my pussy, ever—and yet Dan was watching me and loving it just as much as I was. There was sperm everywhere .... And then it was done.

CHAPTER 19

THE MARITAL SHIFT

∽

EVERYONE HAD ORGASMED. THERE was nothing else that sex could do for us. We had a few content but shy moments before Steve left. This time Steve didn't bother with a shower; I think he learned his lesson there. He just slipped into his clothes quickly and left, sensing our need to be alone. When he left, he shook hands with Dan, respectfully. Then he walked to the other side of the bed where I was sprawled out, and said, "I guess I should shake your hand also." We laughed and then he was gone.

During the next few weeks, Dan went through the strangest transformation. Watching me get fucked so beautifully, hearing me tell him, in no uncertain terms, that he was not capable of the job—it had somehow freed him, just as Cheryl had predicted. Even with all her happy talk about total honesty, I expected Dan to be a basket case if we continued with this. I figured he'd be seriously depressed that he couldn't fully satisfy me, that he'd be insecure in a more devastating way, because it was so clearly the truth.

But that wasn't the case. Instead of trying to prove he was a super stud, Dan realized he could drop that act for good.

His erections started lasting longer. He was more playful, less preoccupied with the hard work of trying to make me cum. He could just have fun with it, be himself. Erections seemed to come more easily to him than before. I was getting off more, too.

Dan even surprised me sometimes. He didn't just want to relive our threesomes. He seemed determined to do with his tongue what he couldn't accomplish with his cock. He ate me out like there was no tomorrow. Once he banged me so hard that the base of his cock slammed me to the point of serious pleasure, even though I could barely feel him inside me. I loved that feeling, but even more, I loved his determination to please me.

Something else happened. Dan started going out every Thursday to play "poker with the guys," or so he said, even though he had never been much of a card player. I knew he wouldn't cheat on me, so that wasn't my concern. But he always came back from those games in such a good mood, which struck me as odd; most guys seem to get into heated arguments during card nights. But hey, if it brought him home in such a good mood, I had no complaints.

A few months later, soon before our daughter was due back in town for the summer, Dan arranged for a girlfriend of mine to pick me up and surprise me with an evening on the town. When we got to the club, I was shocked to see Dan onstage. Dan had gotten back together with band mates from his college days, this time with a new bass player. Those "poker Thursdays" were actually band rehearsals. These guys were pretty good, jamming out a Reggae vibe with some funky/punky interludes. Dan even took some vocals.

There were a few hundred people at the near-packed club. Dan had cashed in a favor; his band was opening for a local favorite. I couldn't help but notice that the girls up front were staring at Dan in particular. He did look really cute. He had his hair spiked up; he didn't look anything like the "corporate

Dan" I was used to. I don't usually care if girls have a crush on Dan, but this time, I found myself keeping a watchful eye. During a break in the set, I clocked a few talking to him. One in particular, a short blonde with small tits busting out of her top, seemed to be laughing at everything he said.

I went over and introduced myself forcefully as "Dan's wife." The girls scattered. Before she walked off, the blond girl gave me the evil eye, one of those "I'll be back" looks. After the show, I cornered Dan and took him straight home. In the car I reminded him, "Remember, you don't get to play. That's not how this works." I was kidding more than anything.

When we got home, I practically ripped his clothes off before we even got through the living room. Jealousy at Dan's groupies had riled me up. I couldn't believe how turned on I was. Dan fucked me good that night. I pulled him into me, feeling his rhythm, loving being his wife, feeling complete. For that night, he was the rock star, and I was his slutty fangirl.

But moods change. Two weeks later, Steve was in town, and Dan was back in a chair, getting another education in how I like to be pleased. I was only too happy to put on a show for him, watching him stroke his cock for me, loving the extent of his devotion, his willingness to expose everything to me. Instead of looking down on him, I looked up to him in a new way. He loved me enough to let me get pleasure elsewhere. And yet, he didn't sulk. Well, not usually. The jealousy drove him to new heights inside and outside of the bedroom. He was determined to excel as a man in any area he could to make our lives better. He was devoted to me. Knowing that freed me to cum all the harder and to love him that much more. What else could I ask?

The path to a good marriage is more uncharted than I realized. I don't know where Dan and I are headed. I don't know if our experiment can survive the test of time and overcome the sheer effort of our daily routines, especially with our daughter home again. I do know that I have changed, and that he has

changed as well. When we threw out all the preconceived ideas
of normalcy we had clung to, we found ourselves.

AN EXPERIENCED AUTHOR WHOSE relationships have evolved from vanilla to anything but, **Alex Hathaway** is fascinated by the erotic power of sexual taboos and the adventures that can be had by exploring them. Alex has a particular interest in writing about cuckolding and the unconventional sexual fulfillment it can provide.

Alex is also the author of *The Education of a Cuckold: A Story of Love, Lust, and Fate.* More novels are on the way.

From Housewife to Cuckoldress is also available as an audiobook.

ALSO BY
ALEX HATHAWAY:

Alex
Hathaway

In this school, the three Rs stand for ruttin', 'rithin', and resignation.

Baby, you're not the cock of the walk.

The Education of a Cuckold

A Story of Love, Lust, and Fate

Jason falls hard for his high school friend Beth, but he isn't confident enough to make his move. When Jason discovers Beth's secret--she is sexually voracious--he also realizes he is too poorly endowed to satisfy her. But wait ... watching her with other men is no small turn-on. Finally, as an adult, he meets Kristen and begins to take his extracurricular studies in submission seriously.